BETH

Michael Edwin Q.

MICHAEL EDWIN Q.

BETH

HE STRIPPED HER OF ALL SHE LOVED:
FREEDOM, HOME, FAMILY, FRIENDS HUSBAND AND CHILD.
NOW, THE ONLY THING TO LIVE FOR IS ... REVENGE!

Published by: ADVANTAGE BOOKS™
                  Longwood, Florida, USA
                  www.advbookstore.com

Library of Congress Catalog Number: 2022934076

1.   Fiction:: African American - Woman
2.   Fiction: African American – Historical
3.   Social Science - Slavery

Cover Design: Alexander von Ness
Editor: nancysabatinicopyedit@gmail.com

First Printing: May 2022
22 23 24 25 26 27   10 9 8 7 6 5 4 3 2 1

1

The Stage is Set

She'd been cursed from birth. From the moment she took her first breath and placed at her mother's breast she was cursed. Oh, not in deformity, but in beauty. For a young black woman, living and working on a plantation in Mississippi beauty was a curse, and Beth was deeply afflicted.

Her eyes like two dark rubies placed over her high cheek bones, her cherub lips like rose petals. If she cared for her hair or not it didn't matter, it always fell in place, crowning her. Willowy arms that swayed like branches at the sides of her long slender torso, held up by legs of Venus. At sixteen years old, there wasn't a women black or white who could hold a candle to her beauty in anyone's memory.

Why would something held so precious by most women be considered a curse? As always the answer is in the question. When you have something precious, many others will want it and try to take it by any means possible.

The life of a slave is nearly impossible. They demand everything you have, sucking the life out of you till they get to the marrow in your bones, and you die young. The more you have to offer, the more they want and the more they will take.

How she stayed a virgin was no mystery and the cause of much of her fear. Obviously, her master preserved her for profit. Someday she would be sold to be some Southern gentleman's mistress, or worse, to a house of ill repute as a prostitute. Remaining a virgin insured the highest price.

Virginity was an oddity on a plantation. Most young women Beth's age were either married and had children or at least been raped. Her priceless beauty protected her for the moment, only to be smothered under the avalanche to come.

Beth's world was small. She lived in a tiny one room shake with her widowed father and her younger sister by four years, Louise.

After the death of her mother, her father took to heavy drink. His name was Thomas, though those that knew him called him Old Tom. He was second generation African, Swahili. Now, two generation from where his family came from, he knew only English and not one word of Swahili. Because of his heavy drinking, his health was not good. He was well liked by all, both slave and overseer. Having what the Irish call a *Touch of the Blarney*, he weaseled his way out of doing any hard labor on the plantation.

Beth's sister, Louise, was a sweet child, never complaining or demanding. She was pretty in her own way, favoring both her parents, making Beth's beauty an oddity in its own way, as she favored neither of her parents.

The one benefit of her beauty, Beth worked at the master's house as a scullery maid. Her days filled with cleaning, be it pots, pans, or plates, or vegetables, meats, floors, windows, and fireplaces. At the end of the day, Beth rushed home to perform many of the duties once performed by her mother: cleaning and cooking. It was a full and difficult day. However, she felt she had no right to complain for it was nothing compared to the work forced on the other slaves. Working cotton damages your body, mind, and spirit, always causing premature death. One look at her younger sister, Louise with her hunched back, torn flesh, and crippled fingers, it was clear to Beth how blessed she was.

Work in the fields started at sunup and stopped at sundown, every day. Though Sunday morning was church time, providing all slaves were at their posts by noon.

Beth and Louise always attended church services. After the death of his wife, once he took to drink, Old Tom, stopped attending. Because of his drinking, his daughters never asked him along, although, they always prayed for his salvation.

The pastor of *Bethel Church,* the only black church in the county, was Reverend Jacob Gaines. Pastor Gaines was a wise and sharp old man, so old there was no one for miles, black or white, who remembered a time when the Bethel Church didn't exist and Reverend Gaines wasn't the pastor.

This plantation mentioned belonged to General Irwin Colby. He earned the title of General during the War of 1812. After the war, he bought one thousand acres with the intent of starting a cotton plantation. Now, forty-five years later, an old man in his late sixties, he'd succeeded in settling the fifth most profitable plantation in the state.

If you asked any of his five hundred slaves if the General was a good man to work for, the answer would vary from slave to slave and from day to day. It all depended on the whims of the old man, and General Colby was a whimsical man.

He was a firm believer in the *Ways of Logic*, a strong and trendy movement at the time. If allowing his slaves Sunday Church made them better workers, then logic guided him to do so. If giving his slaves a day off for a holiday or a wedding kept them a peaceful lot, easier to control, then logic makes it so. When mercy and kindness made the work more efficient, he showed mercy and kindness. As well, if an iron fist seemed in order, it would come down on a slave like an avalanche of rocks, in the form of a whipping to disfigurement or hanging till dead. It all depended on the General's mood that day. Still, most slaves knew it could always be worse.

****

Now the stage is set. We know who and where. Raise the curtain to witness the why and the how. All those of faint heart, easily moved to melancholy, it's time to read no more. We others shall press on. Let the play begin.

2

Royal Blood

Old Tom was a tall, slender, string bean of a man. He was drunk, as he was most days. Walking down the country lane back to the Colby Plantation, he swaggered back and forth across the road. A frightening and unnatural looking scene, like a scarecrow blown about by the wind, only there was no wind that morning.

Every few steps he'd stop, take a flask from his back pocket, take a long pull, swallow, replace the flask, and then continue.

Shaking his head to clear his eyesight, he saw a horsemen approaching. He rushed to the side of the road and hid behind a tree. If it was anyone from the Colby Plantation, and they found him in this condition, he would surely have hell to pay. Probably, a whipping, and although he received a whipping many times, it is not something a person gets use to, and a must to avoid.

As the rider neared, Old Tom recognized him. He came out from hiding and stood in the middle of the road, early enough to not spook the horse.

"Reverend Gaines, long time, preacher," Old Tom declared, his hand up in greeting, wearing a drunkard's warped smile, swaying slightly this way and that.

Reverend Gaines stopped and dismounted.

"Good to see you, too, Old Tom," He said coldly, clearly not pleased with Old Tom's condition.

It seemed strange for the pastor to call him Old Tom. To everyone, Reverend Gaines wasn't just old, he was ancient. The age difference between the two men made Old Tom look like a youngster.

"A little early in the morning, don't you think, Tom?"

"What do you mean?"

"The drinking, Tom, you can barely stand. I smelled you from down the road."

Realizing the cat was out of the bag, Old Tom remained silent. Reverend Gaines continued.

"You haven't been to church in years. I see your daughters, Beth and Louise, every Sunday. You…I see once a year, and when I do you're drunk. What kind of man are you?"

Old Tom looked down at his shoes.

"Look at me when I'm speaking to you," shouted the pastor. "Don't you know who you are? I was here when they brought your grandparents here from Africa. Your grandfather was king of his tribe. There's royal blood flowing through your veins. You married a wonderful woman. Taken away too soon, true, but still it's more than most men could wish for. As well, you have two beautiful daughters. A pack of blessings shower your head, and you throw it all away."

The half smile on Old Tom's face grew to a smile with a full mouth of teeth gleaming at the reverend. He reached into his back pocket, took out the flask, and took a long hard pull on it.

"Ah, that's good," said Old Tom. There was cynicism in his voice. "You know, Reverend, you just called out a long list, and you call them blessings. Maybe from where you're standing. But from where I'm standing they're all good reasons for a man to drink and stay drunk."

With that he took another long pull from his flask, and then tucked it back into his rear pocket.

Hundreds of responses flew through Reverend Gaines' mind. However, if his years taught him anything it was to know where to cast his pearls. If a man has no respect for his past, his family, his children, or even himself, there is nothing you can say to change it. The most you can do is pray someday they have an epiphany.

"Do yourself a favor, Tom. Go off into the bushes, and sleep it off. It would be better to get back to the plantation late and be whipped for it then to be found drunk and then hanged for it."

Even in Old Tom's haze, he knew this to be good advice.

Reverend Gaines mounted his horse, looking down on Old Tom. "If you ever want to talk, you know where I am." With that he traveled on.

Old Tom stood there, watching the reverend ride off. After he was far enough down the road that he was nothing more than a speck in the distance, Old Tom laid down in the grass to the side of the road to sleep it off.

****

"Wake up! Old Tom, ya best be gettin' on!" Dixie Dan shouted as he shook Old Tom to consciousness.

"What do you think you're doin', boy?" grumbled Old Tom.

"Don't ya call me boy, you ain't that much older than me," said Dixie Dan.

Old Tom sat up, looking around like the world was new, and he'd never seen it before.

"Show some respect, boy. Ya know I got royal blood flowin' through my veins."

"All ya got is moonshine flowin' through your veins," laughed Dixie Dan.

"My Grandfather was a king and my Grandmother was his queen," Old Tom countered.

"And your daughter, Beth's worrying about ya. She asked me to fetch ya. I figured I'd find ya here. Now, come on, let me help ya up."

"Unhand me, ya…peasant!" Old Tom shouted.

When Dixie Dan let go, Old Tom fell back down.

"You're like a turtle on his back," laughed Dixie Dan. "Quite griping and let's get ya up."

The short nap did little to sober up Old Tom. He started staggering towards the road. Dixie Dan grabbed hold of him by his shirttail.

"Oh no, ya don't. We're goin' in the backdoor. They see ya drunk like this; they'll whip your hide…that's if you're lucky."

They made their way through the brush till they came to an open field. Tom stumbled over the furrows; getting up onto his feet on his own, most of the time. As they walked on, Tom looked about, realizing something was wrong, he began to laugh.

"Where the hell is everybody?"

"This here is a holiday. The General done gave us all a day off to celebrate Jojoba and Nelly's wedding. Ya done already missed the ceremony. Pastor Gaines was here and everything. He gave them one of his top-notch weddings…had everybody cryin'. Ya should have seen it. We can still get back for the party."

"Party…!" Tom's eyes lit up. "There goin' to be any moonshine at this here party?"

"No, no moonshine. But they got music, and dancin', and plenty of good food. From the looks of it I'd say a hot meal would do ya some good. What ya need is something to eat."

"Eat?" laughed Tom. "No thank you…tried it once…did not like it."

****

As they approached the slave quarters, they heard the festivity and the music. Everyone gathered in the center of the quarters. There were tables filled with food and drink, nothing to the liking of Old Tom, though.

One table in the center of all the other tables sat the newlyweds, Jojoba and Nelly. Being a poor community, guests offered unwanted used furniture, pots, pans, and dishes, for them to start their new life in their new home, a shack no larger or smaller than any other. Folks lined up to wish them well and to kiss the bride.

The musicians played on homemade instruments, the appearance of which looked nothing like the true instruments they mimicked, still, the sound was heavenly and well worth the dance.

A bird's view looking down at the celebration would reveal the gathering was in a circle. This sphere broke up into sections. Older married women congregate in a small group, discussing the concerns of day to day life. Older married men assembled, chatting about this and that of everyday life, as they saw it. Young single women stood in a group waiting for the young single men that stood on the opposite side of the circle to ask them to dance. The young single men eyed the young single women, trying to rally up the courage to ask them to dance.

Within this orb, like a wheel within a wheel, were the dancers. Those that neither worried about such things as attraction and rejection. Life was made for enjoyment. Eat, drink, and be merry, for tomorrow...

When they stepped out of the fields and into the slave quarters, Old Tom took off running. He ran straight into the center of the crowd, in the middle of the dancers. With one hand over his head, he kicked his heels up high, shouting like a madman. Many of the dancers stopped, getting out of his way.

"Why, it's only Old Tom, drunk again!" someone shouted.

The older folk shook their heads in disapproval, the young ones pointing their fingers, laughing at Old Tom. The next moment the dancers picked up where they left off.

Standing with her friends, Beth looked on in disgust and anger. She no longer felt embarrassment; her father played the fool too many times for her to feel humiliated, as everyone knew of his ways and pitied the girl.

Tom staggered through the crowd, stopping in front of the table where the wedding couple sat.

"I want to wish ya all the best, and that all your problems be little ones, if ya catch my drift?" laughed Tom.

"Thank you, Tom," Jojoba said, looking uncomfortable, wishing the old man would go away.

Old Tom lunged across the table at Nelly. "Now, to kiss the bride..." His hands barely touched Nelly, when he landed facedown on the table. Two men, seeing what happened, took hold of Tom.

"Now, now, Tom, it would seem you've had a little too much. Why don't you go on home and sleep it off. Better yet, why don't we bring you home?"

The two men guided him through the crowd towards his shack. Moving in that direction, they came upon Beth. They looked to her with questioning eyes.

"Take him home and toss him on his bed. He'll sleep it off," she told them. "Thank you," she added, turning to her friends, trying to play down the unpleasant incident.

"Get your hands off me, peasant. My granddad was a king! Do ya know what that makes me?"

"A drunk?" one of the men responded. They all laughed, as they walked him up the stairs and across the porch. Inside, they found young Louise adjusting a bow in her hair, prepping for the party. She turned to see who it was. There was no look of surprise on her face. Like her sister, Beth, she'd grown use to it. Her father's drinking was an every day occurrence.

Louise walked to her father's bed and turned down the blanket and sheet. The two men placed Tom onto the bed. It being an awkward moment, they left without saying a word.

"Ya be lookin' mighty pretty today, Beth," Tom muttered with one eye open.

"I'm not Beth, I'm Louise."

He opened the other eye. "That ya are. I can hardly tell the two of ya apart nowadays, as ya growin' so big, and lookin' so more like a lady every day."

Louise smiled. She knew he was having her on. It was his way of complimenting her, and the closest he'd ever come to saying, 'I love you'.

"You want anything to eat?" she asked.

His face scrunched up, as if being stabbed with a knitting needle.

"I'm going to the wedding. Why don't you try to get some sleep?"

With that she was out the door. When she was gone, Tom got out of bed, reached behind the pile of firewood, coming up with a jar of moonshine.

****

"Who are those three?" Fanny asked, pointing across to the other side of the crowd to where most of the young single men stood.

Dahlia slapped Fanny's hand down. "Don't point; they'll know we're talking about them."

"So what…?" Fanny replied. "So what if they know we're interested? Maybe then they'll come and ask us to dance."

She was referring to the three young lads standing across the dance area, eyeing the young women on the other side. It was the Weldon brothers. There was Victor, the oldest, James, one year younger, and two years younger, Gray, each equal in height, weight, and good looks.

General Colby had the good sense to not only give his slaves the day off to celebrate the wedding of Jojoba and Nelly; as well he permitted any friends from neighboring plantations to attend. This, of course, allowed only with their master's consent.

The Weldon brothers were old friends of Jojoba. They were from a plantation miles down the road. Besides the bride and groom, they were the center of attention; especially with the single women of the Colby Plantation.

Interesting, as much as they were being noticed, they too were taking notice, especially of the single women.

"Look, what about those three?" James asked his brothers. "Let's ask them to dance."

"Fine," agreed Victor. "You can have the one that pointed at us. Gray you get the short one, and I'll take the tall good-looking one. She is an angel sent from heaven."

"I wouldn't do that if I were you, friend" exclaimed a young man, one of the Colby Plantation slaves, standing next to them.

"And why wouldn't you…friend?" Victor asked, sounding spoiling for a fight. "Ain't I good enough for her?"

"It's not that," said the young man. "It's because of her beauty that none will approach her."

The three brothers looked bewildered.

The young man continued to make things clearer. "Everyone knows one day the master's gonna sell her as a mistress to some rich white plantation owner. The man who so much as puts a mark on her, let alone damage the goods, that day will be his last."

The three brothers shivered at the thought.

"This is getting us nowhere," declared Victor. "Let's pay our respects to Jojoba and his bride and go home. It's getting late, anyways."

"You two go on. I'll catch up with you later. I'm still hungry. I'm going to get something eat," said Gray.

James looked at his younger brother, following his gaze, which was not in the direction of the food tables. "Like hell you are," said James. "I know what you're hungry for."

Victor placed his hand on Gray's shoulder. "Listen, little brother, don't do anything foolish, and if you do, don't let them catch you. Come on, James, it's a long walk back."

Gray watched his brothers congratulate the bride and groom. With that they started the long hike home.

****

There are times when words fail, unable to express. How often words come up short, and better left unsaid. There are many ways to convey what one wants, a look, a gesture, and definitely the eyes.

Sonnets and songs in their entirety flung across the crowd between Beth and Gray. Once their gazes locked in, they had no eyes for anyone or anything else. They both felt the connection; it was as real as a touch, as a kiss.

His eyes told of her beauty, his yearning for her. Her eyes spoke of trust and surrender, worshipping his chiseled jaw, his dark ebony skin, and his manly features and mannerisms.

As always with the young mind, thoughts of the future come into play. Visions of what it will be like, the bliss, the pleasure, the closeness. Images of years to come spent in wedded harmony and sharing filled their heads. All this happened in the moment of fixing their eyes on each other, all done without words.

The bond sustained as he walked through the sea of dancers, moving towards her. She could already hear his voice in her mind. As he moved in closer, she smiled brightly and obviously at him and him alone. It was his smile to treasure forever.

Then, only a few feet before her everything changed. The warning the young man spoke of, now, flooding his mind, taking over, blocking all other thoughts. Trepidation took hold of him and extinguished the light that shined in his eyes. He walked right passed her.

Beth felt like a sole survivor on a deserted isle watching a ship in the distance passing by, too far to hear her cry for help.

Inwardly, they both were heartbroken knowing what was lost.

She turned to see him walking away from the slave quarters, from the plantation, down the road to catch up with his brothers.

****

It was late in the evening when Beth returned home. There was nothing but red coals in the fireplace. With silver moonlight filling the one-room shack there was no need for her to light a candle.

Once out of her day clothes and into her nightgown, she checked on Louise. The child was nestled comfortably, lost in her dreams. Though asleep, her father, on the other hand, was a tempest under the covers. He twisted and turned, sniffled and coughed, and started moaning as if in pain.

"Papa, are you all right?" she asked softly, gently shaking his shoulder.

His eyes popped open wide, as if someone slapped him on the back of the head, when he realized who it was, calmness took hold.

"Beth, darling," he whispered, closing his eyes once more. "My dear, Beth, all is not as it should be. We are of royal blood. Your great-grandfather was a king in the old country. Slave or not, we are still noble. You're a princess, and need to be treated as one. Don't worry; I'm going to make it all good, again."

"Of course, you are, Papa. Only it's late. Go back to sleep."

Nothing more needed saying, the next moment he was snoring like a bear, as she brought his covers up to his chin.

Resting on her bed, as she drifted off, she remembered the eyes of the young man that almost asked her to dance.

****

Beth woke with a start. Opening her eyes she realized it was still night. The moon had moved to the horizon, no light entered through the one window. The room was dark. Then she heard it, a gentle rapping at the door.

"Who is it?" she asked, low voiced through the door.

"Dixie Dan, open up," came a murmured reply.

She open the door just enough to look out.

"Dan, what are you doing here? It's the middle of the night."

"It's almost dawn," he replied, as if the hour made a difference.

Again, she asked. "What are you doing here, Dan?"

Dixie Dan had the habit of when asked for an answer of taking the long road home.

"I got up from bed, went outside to do my business, as I do sometimes at night. I always try my best not to wake the wife. Well, I get outside, and who do I see coming up the walk, but Mr. Miller, the overseer. I say, 'What ya doin' around here this early in the morning?' He says, 'I be goin' to fetch Old Tom'. 'What for…?' I asked. He says, 'The boss wants him to drive a delivery of chickens into town'.

"Now, I know Old Tom ain't in no condition to drive no chickens. So I say's to Miller, 'Ain't no call to fetch Old Tom, I'll go fetch him for ya, and tell him to make his way to the house'. I figured if Miller saw the state your Pa's in, he'd be in trouble for sure."

"Why didn't you offer to drive the chickens?"

"Oh, Beth, it's near sunup; I gotta be in the fields at first light."

"Thanks for the heads up, Dan."

"Twasn't nothin', Beth, ya have a good day."

She heard him walking off, as she slowly closed the door. She walked over and sat on the edge of her father's bed.

"Papa, you've got to wake up," she said, shaking him gently.

It wasn't any good, he stirred not. She tried not to speak too loudly, as not to wake Louise. She shook him harder and faster, still, he remained asleep.

Nothing left to do other than dress and make the delivery herself.

****

"Where's Old Tom? Where's your father?" Mr. Miller asked Beth.

"I'll do the run for him. He's not feeling well at all."

Miller shot her a side glace of disbelief. They both knew the reason Tom wasn't there. Still, Miller couldn't care less; his orders were to see the delivery made.

"Please, tell the house staff leader I won't be long. I'll be back as soon as I can."

Miller shook his head in compliance.

Beth stepped back to inspect the wagon. The back held one large cage holding at least two dozen chickens. It was a single horse wagon. Beth looked at the horse with apprehension. It was an old chestnut mare with its better years long gone.

Seeing Beth's look of disapproval, Miller defended his choice of horses. "Lilly ain't fast, but she's sure. She'll get the job done. Don't ya worry about Lilly; ya just worry about gettin' these here chickens to market."

The sun was barely up when Beth slapped the reins gently across Lilly's back. Miller spoke true, the mare wasn't fast but she was steady.

A few miles up the road, when she was a ways from the Colby Plantation, coming up on the Townsend property, she heard the sound of distant thunder.

Looking up to the sky, the sun was well over the horizon, the heavens turning their familiar deep blue with not a single cloud in sight.

It didn't make any sense. The booming became louder. She turned on the buckboard, looking behind her. There, down the road were three horsemen racing towards her.

With each passing moment the rumbling grew louder and closer. Lilly stopped, clearly uncomfortable and fearful. Suddenly, when they roared passed, Lilly bolted forward, only to lose her footing. The poor animal stumbled down into a gully on the side of the road. The wagon tipped over, sending the chicken cage ten feet away. Beth was thrown like a stone tossed over the waves of green grass, finally coming to a halt, hitting her head on a rock, falling into unconsciousness.

3

Sanctuary

When Beth came to, she was on the ground staring up at a clear sky of azure. Her head was pounding. Looking about, she saw the wagon; it lay on its side, one of the wheels split in two, another missing. She'd been thrown a dozen yards or more. Working her way to her feet, she inspected herself. Despite a large bump on the back of her head, she seemed fine.

She walked over to the wagon to survey the damage. The first thing she noticed was the cage broke open and all the birds were long gone, leaving only feathers pasted to the wires. Moving to the front, instantly her worse fear was confirmed. Lilly lay motionless, her neck twisted in an unnatural position.

What was to happen, now? If someone other than her did what she did they would be whipped within an inch of their life. This would be considered a mild punishment, as it was just as probable to be hanged or shot.

Excluding Beth, oh no, not Beth! She was far too fair a jewel to tarnish, and too costly a treasure to bury. No, General Colby would want her banished. Waiting for the highest bidder for her charms would no longer be priority. He would sell her as a mistress to the first gentleman to offer a fair amount. Out of his sight and hair, driven away from family and friends and the life she knew.

For a moment, she considered going rabbit, as they called it. Except, few runaway slaves make it far, she being frail her chances were poor and she knew it.

She looked up and down the road. Behind her was the long journey back to The Colby Plantation where the inevitable waited. Up ahead, to the right was the turnoff onto the Townsend Plantation.

When you ask a slave what would be their heartfelt dream. The answer is understandably always the same. To be free! If you were to ask any slave in the county what was their deepest wish, other than freedom, they'd agree it would be to be a slave of the Townsend Plantation.

Mrs. Margaret Townsend, widowed more than twenty years ago, was elderly, frail and crippled, lived her days confined to a wheelchair and her bed, needing constant care. Not many remember when her hair wasn't white and her skin pale as raw bread dough. Much of her time she spent having the Good Book read to her. Though, in the Old and New

Testaments she found no call to not own slaves; although, they swayed her into at least considering the treatment of her slaves.

Slaves at the Townsend Plantation worked ten hour days, as opposed to twelve or more, as expected on other plantations. They received Sundays off as a day of rest, as well as all religious holidays. Good, healthy food was always available and in abundance. There were few whippings, of which never to the point of irreversible physical damage, and never were there any hangings.

If ever there was a place where Beth could find sanctuary it was at the Townsend Plantation, under the protective wing of Mrs. Townsend.

****

Every morning when Beth reported for work, it never failed for her to be awestruck by the grandeur of the Colby Mansion. Now, walking towards the Townsend Mansion, the memory of the Colby home was that of nothing more than a large cottage, charming in its own way. The Townsend Mansion produced images of a fairytale castle with its wrap-around porch, like a protective moat. It was two stories high with a roof of many gables facing in every direction.

She was about to step onto the porch when she heard the sound of galloping hooves. She turned in time to see a lone horseman approaching. Coming closer, she recognized him as one of the riders that earlier spooked Lilly off the road.

He was a strapping example of a young handsome white man, sitting high and erect on his mount. His long hair was light, the hue of freshly cut hay, as was his mustache, which nearly covered his upper lip.

As he rode by, his head turned in her direction, and their eyes met, locking onto each other for just a brief moment and then he rode on towards the barn.

In that short-lived encounter when their eyes met in communion, much was said and learned.

Beth could not help thinking of her encounter with the handsome young man the day before at the wedding. In many ways this meeting of the eyes was the same, yet, deep and disturbingly different.

What Beth sensed in the young man at the wedding was timid innocent attraction and yearning with a strong measure of shyness. She immediately felt attracted and connected with him.

This was poles apart. There was an attraction to the horseman, only in that his physical appearance could not be denied as something grand. Whereas, what his eyes conveyed was formidable, one of wanting at any cost, preferably the cost to others. In that split second she felt he'd stripped her naked and had his way with her.

She immediately reprimanded herself for being so judgmental of someone she didn't know, and evaluating based on nothing more than a glance.

Standing on the porch, she rapped lightly on the door. After no answer, she tried again, still, nothing. A house this size it was highly unlikely that no one was home. She decided to knock again, this time with more force.

The door opened, a short, scruffy looking black woman wearing a full apron stood before her.

'Yes?" the woman asked, looking at Beth most inquisitively.

"I need to speak with Mrs. Townsend, please."

"You do, do you? And you are?"

"My name is Beth Hanley; I'm from the Colby Plantation. I need to speak with Mrs. Townsend."

"And is she expecting you?"

"No she isn't."

The woman sighed long and hard, shaking her head.

"You think Mrs. Townsend's got time for everyone and anybody that can knock on a door. You're mistaken, young miss. You best be on your way." The woman began to close the door. Beth placed her arm out, preventing the door from closing. This didn't sit well with the woman. "Get your arm out of the doorway, or I'll slam it shut."

"No, please, I have to see Mrs. Townsend. It's a matter of life and death," pleaded Beth.

"You're gonna be minus more than an arm, if you don't get off this porch," the woman scolded.

"What's all this about life and death?" a voice called out from within.

"It's nothing, ma'am," replied the woman. "It's just some rude girl from down the road, lookin' for a handout."

"I am not!" Beth shouted into the house. Hoping it was Mrs. Townsend's voice; Beth cried out, "Mrs. Townsend, please, I need to speak with you."

"Well, don't slam the door on the poor girl's arm, Ursula, show her in."

There was no sign of approval on Ursula's face, as she opened the door, letting Beth enter.

In the hallway, Beth found herself confronted with Mrs. Townsend, seated in her wheelchair, a bunch of lace at her throat and wrists, knitting needles and a ball of yarn in her lap.

Mrs. Townsend pointed to the room to her left. "Are you strong enough to push me?" she asked.

"Oh, yes, ma'am," Beth replied, rushing to the back of the wheelchair, guiding it into the room.

"That will be all, Ursula, thank you."

"Yes, ma'am," Ursula called out, stomping off in a huff.

"Put me close to the fire," Mrs. Townsend asked kindly.

There was a roaring fire in the fireplace. Beth couldn't believe anyone would want to sit by a fire on such a warm day. Although, she'd heard many old folk feel a cold that others can't.

Mrs. Townsend gestured her hands about the room. "They call this the 'sitting room'. I think it's funny. For me, every room is a sitting room," the old woman laughed, pointing to the wheels of her chair.

Beth was not too slow as to realize the old woman told a joke, although, she found it to be an awkward one. Still, she smiled and laughed to be polite.

"Tell me, young miss, what is your name?"

"My name is Beth Hanley, ma'am. I'm from the Colby Plantation."

"I know it well," said Mrs. Townsend. "Beth…is that short for Elizabeth?"

"I wouldn't know, ma'am," Beth replied. Strange, Beth never thought of the notion, and honestly didn't know the answer.

"Well, Beth Hanley from the Colby Plantation, how may I help you?"

Beth went solemn, relaying her misfortune, her misgivings of the outcome, and then pleading for sanctuary.

After listening most intensely to Beth's woes, Mrs. Townsend remained silent weighing the pros and cons. When she finished her inner debate, like some Ancient Sage with the Wisdom of Solomon, she announced her verdict.

"My dear child, your story has moved my heart to breaking. You have provoked me to tears. But what am I to do? The simple truth is you are still someone else's property. If I were to take you in, it would be nothing short of theft."

"Please, ma'am, I beseech you. I will be eternally grateful. I will work my fingers to the bone for you every day of my life."

Mrs. Townsend looked near to tears; still, she would not capitulate, shaking her head. "My dear child, it would be theft, and theft is a sin."

"Mrs. Townsend, please…"

"No, my dear, don't you see both our souls hang in the balance. It would be a sin."

"Correct me, if I'm wrong, but the act is not a sin until it's preformed," a male voice called out from the hallway. In walked the handsome young man that Beth saw on horseback only a few minutes ago. He entered the room like a peacock spreading out his full plumage. Standing before them, he continued, addressing Mrs. Townsend.

"Forgive me, Auntie, for listening in, I was just passing by, and I couldn't help overhearing the conversation. I must agree and commend you on your high morals to not take what is not yours. Seriously, there must be an alternative to sending her back home to her doom. If she cannot stay because she belongs to someone else, let us see if we can procure her from her original owner, at a fair price, of course."

"You are most kind, sir," proclaimed Beth.

"You are a smart and good-hearted sort, Collin," said Mrs. Townsend. The old woman smiled with pride towards Beth. "This is my nephew, Collin, my brother's son. He came to me when he was a little boy. I've been surprised by his mind and his heart that are closer to God, more than anyone I know."

Beth curtsied to Collin. "I thank you, sir."

"No need to thank me, young lady, it's the only Christian thing to do. Have no fear; we will see that no harm comes to you."

It was at that moment; Beth regretted ever holding a bad thought about the young man. He was a hero, a saint, a savior. She would trust, believe, and obey every word he uttered. Her heart was moved, and in moving, saw him in a new light, truly handsome.

"Ursula!" he shouted down the hallway. When the woman appeared, he gently gave her orders. "This is Beth. She will be one of our new housekeepers. See that she's given a room, new clothing, and something to eat. She can start work tomorrow." He then turned to Mrs. Townsend. "I'm off to see General Colby, to pay him for this poor woman."

"You seem sure of yourself, Collin?" questioned Mrs. Townsend.

"I am," he replied, "although more so of General Colby's greed."

Before leaving, he smiled at Beth, melting her to soft pliable wax, conquering her completely.

4

A Rock and a Hard Place

"It's been a long time…how've you been, Collin?" General Colby asked, reaching out to shake hands. "Sit, sit," he insisted, pointing to one of the chairs. When Collin sat down, Colby took a seat facing him. "How is your aunt?"

"She's just fine, sir, and thank you for asking."

"Well, you just tell her I was asking about her."

"I will, sir."

"Would you like something to drink?"

"No, thank you, General, I'm just here on a short visit."

"Sounds like business," Colby laughed.

"It is, sir. You have a lovely slave girl named Beth Hanley."

"I did," Colby broke in. "She was to drive a shipment of chickens to market. When she didn't return, we went looking for her. My men found the wagon not far from your place, it was in shambles. It was turned upside down, the wheels were busted, the chickens were all gone, and the horse had a broken neck. I tell you, if I ever get hold of that girl, I swear I'll kill her with my own two hands."

"No you won't. You're not that stupid," Collin said, catching the General's full attention. The man tilted his head, not sure he heard right. Collin continued, "You're a man who knows the value of a dollar."

This compliment soothed the general's demeanor. The man sat back in his chair waiting to hear the rest.

"That girl is beautiful, and I know you've been holding on to her for the highest bidder looking for a mistress, whoever they may be. Except now when word gets out how her negligence cost you so much, you won't be able to give her away. That's why I've come here today. To make you an offer on her so you can recoup your losses."

"She is beautiful," Colby admitted. "That's why I couldn't sell her for less than…"

"Don't play games, General, you're between a rock and a hard place, and you know it. Now, I'm going to make you an offer, it will be fair, and your going to take it."

Colby knew what Collin was saying was true; he sat silently waiting to hear the offer.

"I'll pay you the cost of the wagon, the loss of the chickens and the horse, on top of that, one thousand dollars for the girl."

General Colby smiled. He knew a good deal, when he heard it, and this was a good deal.

"Why are you doing this?" Colby asked.

"Why do you think? You planned to sell her as a mistress, and I am in the market for a mistress."

"Come now, Collin, a young good looking fellow like yourself? Why so much for a slave mistress, when you can have any white woman in the county, married or single? What's your game, Collin?"

"General, you may know much about running a plantation, but you don't know much about men such as I. I don't want what I can have easily. I want what I can't have. Once I get it into my mind I want something, neither God nor man can stop me."

"Maybe so," Colby said, not fully agreeing with Collin's philosophy. "Still, that's a lot of money to spend on just one woman."

Collin laughed. "Don't you worry about the amount I'm spending. I assure you I will get my money's worth."

5

A Moment of Weakness

Beth's accommodations could only be described as a closet with a mattress on the floor. Still, she made it as cozy as possible, sleeping well each night. The clothing given her was the same as all the other women working in the house, black blouse and skirt covered by a full white apron. This was in keeping with the menservants that were dressed in black suits and white shirts.

Though not difficult, the work was plentiful, making for a full day. They received three hearty and healthy meals each day. Although to keep the work flowing constantly, each worker ate their meals alone while the others continued working.

It was this loneliness that weighted heavily on Beth. At The Colby Plantation, she had her family and friends. At the Townsend home, she worked alone, ate alone, and slept alone. Each day there was little contact with anyone. There was never a word of acknowledgment from Mrs. Townsend, and neither hide nor hair of Collin. She understood, being the new girl, it might take time for anyone to warm up to her; however, the temperature remained icy cold.

No one was distrustful or cruel to her. On the contrary, they showed the upmost respect for her. Only, when face to face with anyone, the conversation was always short and to the point, and no further than needed to get across what needed saying. Ursula was the only one that had lengthy words with Beth; however, they were all work related, telling her what chores she must do, and checking on her progress throughout the day.

As weeks past, Beth went as cold as those around her, reluctant to reach out to others, expecting nothing, trudging on in her solitude.

One day, Beth learned it was Ursula's birthday. Not that she was told of this by anyone, it was something she overheard. The good-hearted Mrs. Townsend gave permission for a party to be held in Ursula's honor.

The Townsend property was vast, having many barns, each with its own purpose, all of them scattered about the plantation. The party was to be held in a barn on the farthest end of the property, a good walk from the main house. Of course, they didn't invite Beth.

Inwardly, it hurt Beth – deeply. She tried not to show it and tried to deny it, even to herself.

"What do I care what they do or don't do without me," she murmured under her breath, as she slowly fell asleep on her mattress in her six by four foot room.

She repeated this in her mind like an incantation to ward off evil. She failed miserably.

She decided she would attend the gathering despite not being invited. She'd make one final ditch attempt to make a connection. She'd appeal to their sense of right and wrong, of fairness, of solidarity in slavery and a common heritage.

****

It was more than a mile's walk to the barn. Beth could hear the faint music off in the distance. At the halfway point, she could hear the music clearly. A quarter-mile away, she could hear the laughter and the chatter of the people, the light within the barn shown like a candle in a jack-o-lantern.

Entering the barn, a few heads turned, only to turn away, ignoring her. It was the same when she walked among them, side glances, and then ignoring her completely. The music was loud and joyous. The folks drank, ate, and danced, laughing as if they hadn't a care in the world.

The atmosphere was familiar; striking a chord within, reminding her of the wedding she attended not so long ago at the Colby Plantation. She couldn't remember the wedding without recalling the handsome young man she connected with, only to lose him to memory. His face flashed before her eyes, disappearing like mist, as does all wishful thinking when grounded in dreams and not reality.

Beth saw Ursula standing a few yards away; she tried to catch her attention, only unable to. She made her way through the crowd and towards Ursula. The woman's back was to her. Beth tapped her on the shoulder. Ursula turned, wearing a large smile on her face, which disappeared when she realized it was Beth.

"I wanted to wish you a happy birthday, Ursula."

"Thank you," the woman replied coldly. She remained silent, staring unemotionally at her. Ursula turned her back on Beth, returning to the conversation with her friends. As if by magic, her smile reappeared.

Beth moved about until she fully understood it wasn't by happenstance she was being taken no notice of, this was deliberate. They were intentionally paying no heed to her, casting her out.

She was just about to give in and leave when she spied Ursula and three of her lady friends stepping out the side door for a breath of fresh air. It was a gut reaction, purely, with no thought behind it. Beth felt determined to get to the bottom of it all. Why was she treated in such a manner?

Beth moved through the crowd to the side door. Outside, the world was dark, the stars in the black sky peering through shadowy clouds. Light emitting from within the barn shown out the side door onto the backs of the four women. Beth was too far to hear what they were saying. As she approached, they heard her, stopped their talking, and turned to confront her.

Beth walked to Ursula, looked her in the eye and calmly asked, "Why?"

Ursula looked at her in bewilderment. Beth began to elaborate.

"Why is everyone treating me like this?"

Ursula and the others began laughing. "Listen, you live your life the way you want, we'll live ours. Just leave us alone," Ursula answered.

"I don't understand," Beth replied, truly confused.

The laughter stopped, and there was a long silence. Then, one of the women stepped before Beth, anger contorted her face. "Because you're filth, you're Master Collin's mistress, bought and paid for, and every one knows it."

"That's not true!" shouted Beth. "Mrs. Townsend paid the price for me, to help me!"

"Go away with your lies," growled the woman. "Go back to your fancy man and leave us good people alone."

"You're the one that's lying," Beth hollered into the woman's face.

The woman pulled Beth's arm behind her back, bringing her fist around, slamming into her face. Beth brought her hands up to defend herself, only it was too late. The woman grabbed hold of Beth's hair, pulling her down onto the ground, and jumping on top of her. The two of them wrestled, rolling back and forth, punching, kicking, and biting.

"Catfight!" a man standing at the side door yelled. In less than a minute, most of the folks exited the barn and were now formed into a circle, cheering.

The woman straddled Beth, pinning her to the ground. She took hold of Beth's head, pounding it on the earth.

"Slut…slut," she screamed with each pummel.

Above the clatter of the crowd, the sound of a horse's hooves was heard. Suddenly, a horseman galloped into the center of the circle; it was Master Collin.

"All of you, back into the barn," he shouted as he used his whip on them.

The next moment, only the two women wrestling on the ground remained. Collin reached down, his whip slashing the side of the woman's face. She rolled off Beth, clutching her bleeding cheek.

****

Collin extended his hand, Beth took hold of it. In one quick swoop, he raised her up seated behind him, placing her onto the horse. With another swish of his whip, they galloped off into the dark of night.

It was impossible to see how fast they flew through the night, yet the breeze whooshing around them told of great speed. Beth held on tight to Collin, her head pressed against his back, listening to his deep breaths and pounding heart.

"Please, please, slow down," she cried, her mind whirling with more fear than when in the heat of the fight.

He did more than slow down; he brought the horse to an abrupt halt.

She released her tight grip, removing her head from off his back. He twisted in the saddle, looking over his shoulder at her.

"What was all the ruckus back there about?" he asked.

"I don't get on well with some of the women here. Two of us had words, one thing led to another and…"

He stopped her midsentence, interrupting her, "You're not a good liar. Besides, you don't have the face for it. Now, tell me what happened."

She let out a long sigh. "It seems all the others want nothing to do with me. They say I'm your mistress."

Collin laughed loudly; the sound echoing into the darkness and returning a moment later. "My mistress…? And what's wrong with that?"

"Well, for one thing, it's not true."

He stopped laughing, yet didn't answer.

"Is it?" she asked shyly.

"You know I did it to help you. You were there; you knew my intentions."

Now she felt ashamed. "I'm sorry. They've got me all upset; I'm not thinking straight."

Taking his feet out of the stirrups, he brought his leg over to be able to turn sideways in the saddle and face her. "If you were my mistress, would it be so bad?"

"I'm not that sort of girl, sir."

"Don't you find me attractive?"

"Yes, I do but…" She stopped for a moment, realizing she had said the wrong thing at the wrong time. She'd given herself away. Beth continued, trying to repair the damage. "You're a fine looking man, sir. It's not you, sir, it's me. I can't see me being anyone's mistress."

"Saving yourself, are you?"

"Yes I am, sir."

Her answer not only surprised him, it stopped him in his tracks. He took a few seconds to refocus. He decided to try a different approach.

"Don't you think we've grown close enough for you to give up calling me *sir*?"

She smiled. "Very well, Collin…" she said, casting her eyes downward.

He lifted her chin up. "No need to be so shy." They smiled at each other. "Now, this is the second time I've saved your life. Don't you think that merits a kiss?"

Not wanting to argue the matter, she reached up and kissed him on the cheek.

He laughed, "A peck, indeed. You kiss like my auntie. You are a shy one, aren't you? Never mind, we'll change that in time."

Feeling extremely uncomfortable, Beth made an effort to change the subject.

"Where are we?" she asked.

The dark was all around and a fog was moving in, limiting visibility.

"I have no idea," he laughed.

This did not calm her in the slightest. "What are we to do?"

"There's not much we can do," he answered. "We can ride around in the dark, hoping we come onto a recognizable landmark or we can wait until sunup and find out our way back in the light of day. I suggest we wait for the dawn."

This was not what she wanted to hear.

He hopped off the mount to the ground. Reaching up, he helped her down. He tied the horse to a bush. Taking a blanket from the back of his saddle, he spread it out on the ground.

"Lay down, we can wait for sunrise, here."

She looked at him like he'd asked for her soul.

"Go ahead, lay down. I promise you that you will be unmolested."

Taking him at his word, she lay down on the blanket. On her side, she closed her eyes. He too got down on the blanket. The last thing she remembered, before she fell asleep, was his voice in her ear. "Don't worry, one day you will want me to have you."

****

Can you remember your moments of weakness, lost in the instant, can any of us really point a finger?

The sun was coming over the horizon, the world still dull and colorless, yet, strangely illuminated. Beth woke from the pressure of Collin's body upon her. His lips pressed on hers, his hands roving over her faster than she could protest. And she did protest, however, thinking of it later her objections were weak and lame, for there was a part of her that wanted this as much as he.

In time she succumbed to his wishes. Letting down her guard, allowing him to have his way, for it became her way, as well.

Without warning, there came a moment when she was all his completely, wanting it never to stop. That is when it all stopped.

They remained on the blanket in silence. Both of them breathing deep and heavy, Collin's face buried into her neck. Beth stared up at the sky, it slowly turning blue, as the stars vanished.

Collin rose, looking around, he knew where they were. Standing over her, buttoning his trousers, he spoke, his words crashing down on her like a hammer to an anvil.

"See, that wasn't so bad, now, was it? Get yourself together; we still have a ways to go."

"That's all right, I'll walk it," she replied.

"Don't be silly, it's still quite a ways on."

"Please, I need to be alone."

"It was your first time, wasn't it?" he said in a half laugh. "I've heard that women, when it's their first time, get moody. Very well, give me the blanket, I'll ride on ahead, and tell them you'll be there soon."

"No, don't tell them anything," she pleaded in a low voice.

"Oh, yes, of course," he giggled.

After the sound of the horse's hooves was in the distance, Beth began walking. She felt ashamed and foolish. The things she'd been accused of, all that she denied and fought against were now true. Everything they pointed their fingers at her of being, she now was. Every evil name they called her was now spot on.

6

One Lucky Girl

Beth withdrew within herself, her sorrow showed in her eyes making them look like murky water after a storm, which went unnoticed by all those around her. The other slaves avoided her, much less looked at or acknowledge her.

As for her relationship with Collin, it became an unholy alliance, a bond of master and slave, a demonic union. Something died within her the night she spent with Collin, and whatever was left of her was slowly fading.

There was a power over Beth that Collin possessed; one she neither understood, nor could she deflect. Just being in his presence would empty her of all thought and emotion, a ragdoll, his plaything.

During the day while she was working, he'd often sneak up on her from behind, grab her tightly and molest her till they heard someone approaching or his aunt calling for him. Beth would go limp, staring at the ceiling. No looks or words were ever exchanged.

Some nights he'd come to her room and have his way with her. Again, no words were spoken. Beth would close her eyes and think of nothing. She kept a bucket and a towel next to her bed to clean herself with. Then she'd cry herself to sleep.

****

Since living and working on the Townsend Plantation, not once did Beth step into the slave church. Each Sunday, she spent her time in prayer and mediation, only not in church. She knew what she'd find. Surely, there would be the other slaves from the Townsend Plantation. She knew what they thought of her. She could take them ignoring her: however, the cold stares of hatred, yes, hatred in a church; that would be too much for her.

As well, there'd be slaves from the Colby Plantation, people who knew her well, childhood friends. Surely, they heard of her life at the Townsend Plantation. She couldn't face their ridicule. Of course in attendance would be her younger sister, Louise. It would break her heart knowing her sister knew.

Understand, there are as many reasons to go to church as there are people. Especially, other than what you think there are. Some come to see, others to be seen, some to refresh themselves, or strengthen for the coming week. Those with guilty consciences come to beg forgiveness, find solace. There are those who find life easier to just following the others, flow with the current and not fight it, not to stand out. There are so many reasons to go to church other than praise, worship, learning and fellowship.

Sadly, there is another reason people go to church. One so unchristian, it stands out from all the others, and sorrowfully most prevalent, and that is *Gossip*.

Jealousy is the green-eyed monster, and gossip is his unholy servant, his demonic messenger. This is what Beth feared the most about going to Sunday service. Still, after a day of prayer and fasting, her inner voice directed her to church.

****

She came late, the church was full. Everyone singing hymns, many with their eyes and hands raised to heaven.

Standing at the back of the church, that's when many heads turned, eyeing her every move, several faces casting that judgmental look that cut into Beth's heart.

She was determined to ignore it all. She would trudge forward till she found her sister, Louise, and sit with her.

She found Louise sitting in the third row from the front. She politely moved across the pew to sit with her sister. Louise was surprised; she smiled, moving over to give Beth room. The look on Louise's face was nothing to the amazed look on Beth's, for seated next to Louise was their father. That's right, Old Tom, only now he was sitting up straight, stone-cold sober. He was as clean as his clothes, his face shaved and his hair cut. He leaned forward; turned to smile at Beth, finishing with a wink of his eye.

From that moment on, Beth was lost in thought. She sang none of the hymns, heard nothing of the sermon. Paying no mind of the others, her thoughts and eyes were always on her sister and their father.

When Reverend Gaines finished and the church began to empty, Beth turned to her family. Not giving her time to ask, Tom answered all of Beth's questions.

"I found religion, Beth. Ain't it wonderful? I've been saved! I ain't had a drop to drink in I don't know how long. It was all your sister Louise's doin'. She invited the Reverend Gaines to the house for dinner one night. The man gave me the hardest longest ear bangin' a person could withstand. Don't know what it was, but when all was said and done and the dust cleared, I was saved."

"How have you been, Beth?" Louise asked, wanting to steer the conversation to her sister. Beth couldn't help noticing the once little girl was now transforming into a young woman.

Beth's first impulse was to lie, and say that everything was fine, except, just the thought of her predicament could bring her to tears. So she changed the subject, redirecting the focus of the conversation back to her father.

"You look good, Papa. I've never seen those clothes on you before. You both look good." This was also a roundabout way of asking how they could afford such fine clothes.

"Your beau, I mean Collin Townsend. He sends us money nearly every week. We've been not only able to survive, but to live well, for once in our lives," Tom answered.

To say Beth was shocked to hear this was an understatement. Her father continued.

"Mr. Townsend buying you and takin' you under his wing like he did has been a godsend. Tell him thanks from us when you see him, again."

It was then Beth understood what game Collin played. He did nothing out of the kindness of his heart, assuming he had a heart. He certainly didn't shower gifts on her family for his love of her. There was no love between them. No, this was his way of saying I can make your life as good or as miserable as need be. So, do as I say.

"Speaking of Mr. Townsend, I need to get back," Beth announced, rising from her seat and stepping out of the pew.

"Wait, we'll walk with you," said Louise.

As the three walked out of the church and into the light, Beth saw her friends, Dahlia and Fanny standing under a tree, waving for her to come.

"I'm sorry, Papa, Louise, I see some friends I need to speak with."

"As long as you promise to come to church more often, so we can see you," said Louise.

"Of course, I will," replied Beth.

Her father took hold of her, kissing her cheek, and then whispering in her ear. "I love you so much, girl. I'm so happy and proud of you."

She knew he meant well, still, it was the wrong thing to say to Beth at this time in her life.

"I have to go," said Beth as she walked away.

Dahlia and Fanny rushed to her. They fell into one another's arms, laughing.

"Girl, you look so good!" Dahlia remarked. "Don't she look good, Fanny?"

"Like a princess."

"You know, Beth," said Dahlia, "you're the envy of every girl at Colby's. You're all they ever talk about."

"I wish the girls at Townsend Plantation thought the same, they're not very friendly."

"The girls here at Colby would probably treat you even worse. Like I said it's all about envy. They're all jealous."

"But we still love you," remarked Fanny.

"Tell you what, if that Collin Townsend ever needs another lady friend, you send him this way, you hear." remarked Dahlia.

"You can count me in, too," said Fanny.

"Let me take another look at you," Dalia said backing off to take in a full view of Beth. "Oh, Beth, you sure are one lucky girl."

Beth forced a smile. "Yeah, I'm one lucky girl."

7

Poignant

Life moves slowly when it has no point, and Beth's life was pointless. Her days were filled with emptiness. There was the weight of having nothing to share, and no one to share it with, even if she had.

Though Collin's late night visits to her room became less frequent, they still continued. This made for more sleepless nights, not knowing that at any moment he'd enter and have his way.

Her attendance at church, Sunday service, also became infrequent. If God is love, certainly he could never love her. She was not worthy of love by him or anyone else.

She'd miss seeing her father and sister; nevertheless, she couldn't bear the shame she'd endure from the others at church.

If she even believed that God would so much as acknowledge her, she would have prayed to die.

****

Beth was quite young when her mother died. Raised by her father, a drunken one at that, proved to have many disadvantages. The absence of a woman figure in her life left her guessing about much needed information that can only be handed down from one generation to another.

There was much talk about this and that. Only time would prove them true or false. Beth was about to learn of one.

Though Ursula held no love for Beth, she was the one to set her straight. Nausea came over Beth, surprisingly and suddenly. Unable to control herself, Beth rushed out the kitchen backdoor. Ursula found Beth outside; the poor girl bent over, pressing her hands on the side of the building, as she vomited onto a flowerbed.

Ursula burst into a fit of laughter, pointing at the young woman. "See, that's what ya get."

"The milk must be spoiled," Beth said, barely able to get the words out.

Ursula laughed louder and harder. "You're the only thing spoiled in this house, my dear. You little slut, now you're goin' to get what you deserve."

Beth slowly stood up, taking her hands from the wall, and then wiping her mouth across the back of her hand. "I don't understand. What are you saying?"

Ursula spoke between laughs. "You got the morning sickness, you stupid girl."

"What's that?" asked Beth. "Is it some kind of disease?"

"A disease!" laughed Ursula. "Yeah, there's a lot of that goin' around." Ursula was laughing so hard she choked. "There's only one way to get it, too. Looks like you got a bad case of it."

"What disease? What's the cure," asked Beth, feeling another surge of nausea coming over her.

Once more, Beth pressed her hands on the wall, bent over, and wretched onto the flowerbed.

"You're goin' to have a baby, you ignorant girl. That's what the morning sickness tells ya. Mark my word, you'll regret the day you came to Townsend. Ain't no use in guessin' who the father be. Wait till Mrs. Townsend learns of this, she'll disown her nephew, and she'll sell you faster than ya can say Jack Robinson. That is if she or Collin don't kill ya first."

****

Old Mrs. Townsend became more unaware of her surroundings with each passing day, as age quickly overshadowed her.

The male servants carried Mrs. Townsend downstairs. A wheelchair waited for her; they brought her into the dining room for her breakfast. Though she always sent an invitation to her nephew, she usually dined alone.

This was the time of day Beth would go to Mrs. Townsend's bedroom, straighten up, change the bedding and make the bed. When she finished, she'd gather the used sheets up in her arms and take them downstairs.

This one particular day, as she walked down the hallway towards the stairs, Collin snuck up behind her, grabbing her. The man was like an octopus, his many tentacles exploring her.

Normally, she would close her eyes and shut down her mind, remaining motionless and breathless till he's had his fill and walked away. This day was different.

"Please, don't," she murmured.

At first he heard nothing. She repeated her plea many times before it even registered in his mind.

To Beth's dismay, when her words finally found their way to his brain, it had the opposite affect. Instead of extinguishing the flame of his desire, it was as if she threw kerosene on it. He was beside himself with passion, a hungry beast driven only by instinct.

"Please, Collin, stop it! I'm going to have a baby, your baby!"

Still holding her tightly, he stopped his motion. She never as much as called him Collin, let alone make a demand of him. As well, the content of the sentence gave him pause.

"What are you saying? Are you joking with me?"

Beth turned around to face him. "Does this look like I'm joking?"

One look and he knew she was in earnest.

"How do you know it's mine?" he asked.

"I know it's yours, as you know it is. Besides your aunt, everyone on the plantation knows what's been going on between us. There isn't a slave who will so much as look at me or speak to me, let alone touch me. You know as well as I do, it's your child."

He released her, backing up a few steps. "Well, I just can't have that. We'll have to do something about it."

"What do you mean?" she asked fearfully.

"I mean, I'm not going to allow this. There are ways of dealing with such problems."

"Over my dead body," she sneered.

"That is one possibility," he said, smiling a crooked smile.

"You try anything, I'll tell your aunt; I'll tell Mrs. Townsend," Beth warned with the utmost seriousness.

He began laughing uncontrollably.

"You actually believe you have any power in this matter. Go ahead, open Pandora's Box, tell my aunt. You have no idea what troubles are ahead."

Wearing a smile he'd borrowed from the devil, Collin backed away down the hall. "Love you," he said, blowing her a kiss, and then disappearing around the next corner.

****

Days passed, Beth went about her work without a sign of Collin. She couldn't say which was worse, him sneaking up on her without warning or to constantly worrying when he would. It was the same at night. On her bed, sleep became nearly impossible, suspecting he might crash through the door at any moment. It wasn't till the middle of the night would she fall asleep from exhaustion. The next night would be the same.

It was one particular morning, one dark and gray morning with clouds so dense the sun was blotted from the sky. It felt like the night finally conquered the world and the day would never start.

Ursula's early morning duty was to wake Mrs. Townsend and help her get ready for the day. After which she would return downstairs to the kitchen to prepare breakfast. Then two of the stronger slaves that worked at the nearby barn came to the house, went upstairs to carry the old woman down to the dining room. However, this morning was different.

It was the time of morning when Beth took fresh linen up to Mrs. Townsend's room and changed the bedding. When she passed the kitchen, clean folded sheets in her arms, Ursula stopped her.

"Where you goin'. . .?" Ursula asked, standing in the kitchen doorway.

Beth looked at her, bewildered. "Upstairs to change Mrs. Townsend's sheets, like I do every morning."

"Not today. The poor woman's not feeling well. Put those sheets back. I want you to take her breakfast up to her."

Beth went back to the linen closet and deposited the sheets. When she returned, Ursula was at the kitchen doorway holding a food tray.

"You think you can get this upstairs without dropping it all over?"

Beth learned not to go back and forth with Ursula, it never turned out well. In silence, she took the tray from Ursula and headed towards the stairs.

"Move it, the eggs will get cold," Ursula called out. Again, Beth ignored her.

Beth moved carefully and slowly upstairs. Entering Mrs. Townsend's bedroom, Beth placed the tray on a table. She walked over to the bed to help the woman into a sitting up position.

"I've brought you your breakfast, ma'am," Beth said softly.

Mrs. Townsend's eyes fluttered slightly.

"Ma'am, I brought your breakfast."

There was a gurgling sound coming from deep in the woman's throat. Again, her eyes quivered, as if she wanted to open her eyes, yet she couldn't.

"Ma'am, are you all right?" Beth asked, taking hold of the old woman's shoulder and shaking it slightly.

She murmured, trying to speak, still, no words came from her. Her lips moved slightly, as spittle dripped from the sides of her mouth.

Fearing the worst, Beth ran from the room, downstairs to the kitchen.

"There's something wrong with Mrs. Townsend," Beth shouted in the doorway.

Ursula ran past Beth, up the stairs, and into the bedroom. Beth was close behind. Ursula rushed to the bedside. Beth stood in the doorway looking worried.

With a handkerchief she found on the nightstand, Ursula wiped the sides of the woman's lips. Then she placed her hand on Mrs. Townsend's forehead, checking for fever.

Ursula turned to Beth. "Go to the barn; tell them to go fetch Dr. Carson!"

Beth spun around and dashed downstairs. She heard Ursula shout, "Hurry!"

****

Dr. Carson was not the closest doctor; however, he was the best. The only doctor Mrs. Townsend would see. He'd been the family doctor for more than twenty years. He was a short, forgettable man with milky eyes, a bald head, and white beard.

He rushed to Mrs. Townsend's bedside, placing his black leather bag on the bed.

There was a wet towel on the old woman's forehead. Dr. Carson removed it and held it up for all to see.

"Who did this?" he shouted.

"I did," Ursula confessed shyly. "She was burning up; I figured it would cool her down."

"Old wives' tales," he barked, tossing the wet towel at Ursula.

Just then, Collin appeared at the door. "How is she?" he called to Dr. Carson.

"I don't know, yet. I want all of you to clear out, and let me do my job."

"Even me?" Collin asked.

"Even you," Dr. Carson hollered. "All of you out this instant!"

After closing the door, Collin remained in the hallway.

"Don't you two have better things to do?" he said, addressing Beth and Ursula.

The two women started down the stairs.

"I put my hand on that old woman," said Beth, "she was burning up. You did the right thing by putting a cool towel on her. That doctor has no right to talk to you that way."

Amazing how much a little sympathy can matter, and how far it can go. Ursula looked at Beth. The ocean that separated them was now a thin trickle no wider than your thumb.

****

An hour later, they heard footsteps on the stairs. Collin appeared in the doorway of the kitchen, Dr. Carson standing behind him.

"I'm afraid it's bad new," said Collin. "My aunt, Mrs. Townsend, has passed away."

A look of shock washed over Beth's face. Ursula brought her apron up to her face, and began to cry into it.

"Go tell the boys at the barn they need to go to the family plot and dig a grave. I want it ready early tomorrow morning," Collin ordered.

He and the doctor left, walking to the front door.

Ursula looked up with tearful eyes. "Be a good girl, Beth. You go tell the men at the barn what to do. I just can't…"

"It's all right, Ursula. I'll take care of it," Beth said, walking to the back door.

When they heard the barn door open, the men stopped what they were doing and jumped to attention. When they realized it was only Beth, they relaxed.

"Got bad news," Beth announced. "Mrs. Townsend is dead. Master Collin told me to tell you men to go to the family plot and dig a grave for her. He wants it ready by early morn."

Looking into their faces, she realized it made no never mind to them. The old woman's passing meant nothing. It didn't matter who was in charge, nothing would change for them. Today was just like yesterday, and it would be the same tomorrow.

Leaving the barn, Beth looked to the front of the house. Dr. Carson was in his buggy, speaking with Collin standing beside the carriage. She was too far to hear what they said; however, she could see them clearly.

Collin reached into his jacket, took out a large envelope, and handed it to the doctor who nodded his thanks. The doctor slapped the reins and drove off.

Walking back to the house, Beth thought about what she'd just saw. It was understandable Collin would pay for the doctor's services. Only, how could Collin know the doctor's fee in advance, and have it ready before time, and why was it in an envelope? Something wasn't right.

8

Changing of the Guard

The Townsend family plot was a half mile from the house. It was a large area, as if someone predicted the Townsend Plantation and family would go on forever. A waist-high white picket fence surrounded it. The grave for Mrs. Townsend was ready, deep and wide, next to the grave of her husband.

The fenced in area was filled with guests, neighbors, friends, and church members. Outside the barrier, they allowed the slaves to come and pay their respects. Though it wasn't mandatory, all Townsend Plantation slaves gathered, fearing an absence would be questioned later. Some of them shed tears. If it was for show or true sadness, it was difficult to say. The true answer is hidden in the heart.

No one spoke. Only the sound of the wind filled their ears. The rickety old wagon carrying the coffin coming slowly up the path broke this near silence.

The coffin was large, made of rich wood, with brass handles. Mrs. Townsend bought it from a catalog just after her husband passed. It remained in the attic all these years. It took four strong men to get it down.

The same strong men took the coffin from the wagon, onto the family plot, and lowered it down into the grave.

The Reverend Jacob Riley from the First Lutheran Church of Sussex rode all the way from downtown to give the eulogy. Beth was too far from the grave to hear a word of it; still, she could see everything clearly. She never took her eyes off Collin.

He stood at the edge of the grave, his head bowed, staring into the dark hole. His face was without expression, making it impossible to read his thoughts. Was he sad to lose his aunt, after all she was his only living relative? Or was he glad to be rid of her, since he would inherit all that was hers. Of course, the first was possible, yet improbable. He already had full control of the plantation and all her money, all the power was his. She was elderly, and sure to die soon, anyway. All her death meant was a transfer of names on paper.

Then a frightening thought came on Beth. Was it just a coincidence that Mrs. Townsend's passing occurred just after she warned Collin that she was willing to tell his aunt about them and the baby? Mrs. Townsend believed firmly in her own moral code. Who could say what her reaction to Collin having his way with one of the slaves might be? What would be her view on him conceiving a child with a slave? How would she react? Sure, he wheeled the power in the family, except everything was in her name, giving her the ability to remove that power from his hands. Was Collin willing to take that chance?

She remembered the incident out front of the house, Collin handing Dr. Carson a large envelope. Was it payment for evil services? It appeared Mrs. Townsend died of natural causes. Only, wouldn't that be a simple illusion for a doctor with so many chemicals at his disposal to perform? Wouldn't it be an easy task for the one person that made out the death certificate?

Shame and fear came on Beth, shame, to think that again just her presence caused havoc and sorrow, and fear, for now there was no stopping Collin's lusts. Before he was obliged to keep his hungers in check and to himself, now there would be nothing to hold him back and nothing to hide. All the neighbors and all on the plantation knew what kind of person he was. Yet, did it matter to them what he did in his private life, as long as it didn't affect them. If he wanted to lose his soul, what was it to them?

Before the ceremony was over, the slaves were given word they were to return to their work. The kitchen staff, including Beth, returned to prepare food for the guests. It isn't a funeral without something to eat.

Guests filled the entire first floor of the house, elbow to elbow. Ursula and one of the other women were in the kitchen preparing the food and drinks as fast as they could. While Beth and two others walked about with trays offering the fare to the guests, devouring the food and drinks as fast as it could be served to them.

The dim of so many people in conversation made it nearly impossible to hear one word. Not that Beth cared about what they had to say. That is until she spotted Dr. Carson standing alone in the far corner of the room. She walked towards him.

What could she say? What could she ask? She only knew she needed to speak with him.

With only a few steps to go, one of the guests took the last morsel of food off her tray. She felt a tapping on her shoulder. She turned to be confronted with Collin.

"Shouldn't you be getting back to the kitchen for more food?" he asked in a friendly tone.

She nodded and started to leave the room, but not without looking back over her shoulder. Collin approached Dr. Carson, gesturing with his hand for the two of them to step out of the crowd for a private talk.

The kitchen was a whirlwind of confusion, as Ursula and the others tried desperately to keep up with the demand. Quickly, Beth filled her tray with more food and walked out. In the hallway she heard voices, men's voices, talking at a turn down the hall. She recognized Collin's voice. As softly as she could, she walked as close as she deemed safe to hear.

"My good doctor, I've already paid you, and handsomely, I might add."

"I'm not disputing that, Collin. My services were paid in full. What I'm talking about is hush money. You want me to keep my mouth shut, don't you?"

"Might I remind you, it was under my orders and paid for by me that the old girl is dead. However, you were the one to make it happen. We are both in it up to our necks."

"Collin, I'm a doctor; I'm a wonder with drugs. I could have your aunt exhumed and prove you were the one that killed her."

There was a short pause in his speech, and then he continued.

"Listen, Collin, I'm not trying to make your life miserable. Just give me a little taste more and we'll never have this conversation again."

"How do I know this won't be a continuing thing and that you won't come back again and again asking for more?" Collin asked.

"I'll be honest with you," returned the doctor. "I'm getting old, I desperately want to retire. Settle back and live the rest of my life in peace. This is why I took your offer in the first place. Only, after looking at my finances, I'm afraid I come up a bit short. Now, if you could just make up the difference of say…one thousand…you'll never hear from me again."

"Very well," answered Collin. "I don't keep that amount of money on hand. I'll get it to you in a day or two."

"I appreciate it, Collin. I promise you; another thousand and I'll be out of your hair."

With that, Dr. Carson exited the alcove, walking down the hall, away from Beth. He never saw her. It was much different with Collin. He turned the corner, only to confront Beth face to face.

A look of terror swept over her.

"Don't you have something better to do?" Collin snapped at her.

She nodded, walking off into the next room.

****

It was a common fact that most black slaves in the South couldn't read or write. Understandable, as it was illegal in most states to teach reading and writing to a slave. Still there were instances where some learned the skill, for whatever reason. There were masters who trusted certain slaves to buy and sell for them during their absence. These slaves needed to read or write a bill of sale. There were also white families with older family members that needed constant care. A slave that could read to the elderly or bedridden was a godsend. There were many other reasons, as well.

The slaves at Townsend Plantation were no exception. Few knew any of these skills. However, one of the few that did just happened to be Ursula. She was taught purposely to read to Mrs. Townsend when the old woman's eyesight began to fail her. After years of reading to Mrs. Townsend, Ursula became extremely good at it.

Ursula and Beth sat in the kitchen, drinking coffee. Ursula read the newspaper that eventually would end up on the dining table for Collin to read with his breakfast.

"My Lord, will you look-e-here," Ursula exclaimed.

Beth jumped from her seat, rushed around the table to stand behind Ursula, looking over her shoulder at the newspaper, not knowing one word from another. "What does it say?" Beth asked.

Ursula looked up from the paper to Beth. "You remember that nice doctor that came to look over Mrs. Townsend the day she died, the one that came to the funeral?"

"Yes, I remember him. What about him?"

"Well, it says here the poor man is dead."

A chill ran up Beth's spine. There was no doubt in her mind someone murdered the doctor, and the culprit was Collin. She felt tempted to confide in Ursula, and then decided not to. The less anyone knew the better.

"What does it say? Read it to me," Beth asked like a child wanting to open a birthday present.

Ursula returned to the newspaper, reading the article aloud, slowly, carefully, and clearly.

CHANGING OF THE GUARD
By
Ralph Maynard

There are few, if any, people that remember a time when Doctor Renton Carson was not part of our community and one of the most well known and sought out doctors in the county.

However, time stands still for no man. Sad to say, the good doctor passed away in his home this past Thursday from complications brought on by a fall down a flight of stairs.

Doctor Carson was looking forward to his retirement this coming July.

A memorial will be held at the First Lutheran Church of Sussex this Saturday at ten in the morning.

Doctor Carson is survived by his loving wife, Justine, and their son Gregory, our thoughts and prayers go out to them.

****

When she finished reading, Ursula folded the paper, handing it to Beth.

"Here, place it on the dining room table. The master's expecting it with his breakfast."

Taking the newspaper, Beth rushed to the dining room, placing it down at the head of the table next to the setting. All of a sudden, Beth heard Collin descending the stairs. She was afraid to meet him face to face. Surely, he knew that she knew. She ran back into the kitchen, perspiration forming on her brow, her breathing quick and heavy.

Ursula took notice of her. "Beth, what's the matter with you, girl. You're look like you've been running from the devil."

9

Any Bright Ideas

Beth lived in fear, waiting for the day Collin would destroy her. She was a problem for him that needed eliminating, and they both knew it. Question was when and how. She had the goods on him. She'd heard the conversation between Collin and Dr. Carson. A day later, the doctor was dead. Even a child can put two and two together.

To make matters worse, she was carrying his baby. Collin coldly said that she having the baby would never happen. She was not showing, yet. However, when she did begin to show, he was sure to take action – only how?

Early one morning, Beth entered the kitchen. Ursula was there alone. She stood with tears in her eyes, holding her hand out to Beth, handing her a sack.

"Master Collin wants you to pack your things, and then meet him outside," Ursula mournfully announced.

Nothing more needed saying. They both knew this was not going to end well.

"I'm sorry we got off on the wrong foot," Ursula confessed. "I'm gonna miss you."

"I'll miss you, too," said Beth, taking the sack from Ursula and leaving the kitchen.

In her room, Beth placed a change of clothing into the sack. Walking out the front of the house, Collin sat on the driver's side of a one-horse wagon, waiting.

She knew what he wanted. Without a word, she hoisted up, sitting beside him.

Collin wanted to be rid of her; except, how was he going to do it? Beth could only think of two scenarios. He could sell her to another plantation, or he could kill her.

A few feet from the house was a dirt road. If he steered to the right it would take them to the main road. That meant he was taking her to another plantation to be sold, or to town where there was a weekly slave auction. Except, he took a turn left heading deeper into the property. There was a good chance he planned to kill her. Then why would he have her pack her belongings? Was it to give her a false sense of safety?

They rode past the fields of cotton, each with slaves tending or harvesting, and then past the slave quarters, after which the road led into the forest.

When the trees were all around and the fields far behind, Beth began panicking inwardly. Collin's jacket was unbuttoned; she could see his pistol strapped to his side. She thought about jumping from the wagon and making a run for it. That would surely mean a bullet in the back. She would not get far. Her only hope was to keep her wits about her, and wait for an opportune moment of which she held no idea what that might look like.

As they rode deeper into the forest, the overhead foliage became thick, blocking out the sunlight. It was nearly impossible to tell the exact time of day, the darkness making greens and whites gray, and browns black.

Looking up ahead, Beth saw a small structure. Coming closer, she realized it was a small one-room cabin.

Collin stopped the wagon and pointed. "I often stay here when I'm hunting, especially in the winter. I want you to stay here until you have the child. After that, we'll figure what to do."

Beth didn't know what to think. Part of her felt relieved, while another was filled with dread.

Collin jumped down from the buckboard, went to the back of the wagon to fetch a crate of groceries she hadn't noticed.

"Well, come along," he ordered.

She jumped down, and followed him into the cabin.

It was as she suspected; it was only one-room. It was all clean and neat. Against the farthest wall was a large bed. In one corner was a potbelly stove with a small pile of wood next to it. There was a table with two chairs, pots and pans, a nightstand by the bed on which was a kerosene lamp and a small barrel of water off in the opposite corner.

"It's not much," said Collin, placing the groceries on the table. "But you can live comfortably here." He pointed to the bed. "There's a chamber pot under the bed, for when you've got to do your business. Try not to use too much of the water for cleaning as much as drinking," he said, motioning to the small water barrel. He opened the door, starting to exit. "I'll be back every few days with food and fresh water." With that, he walked out, closing the door.

She heard the clicking of a padlock. She rushed to one of the windows only to see Collin ride off. That's when she noticed the bars on the windows.

****

By the next day, Beth understood what she was in for, long tedious hours. She eventually took to walking the room, back and forth, wall to wall, and then in circles, going left and then right. She'd stare out the widows for hours. Just the view of a bird or a squirrel was cause for celebration. When she needed to sit, it was always on one of the chairs, never the bed. She learned that sitting on the bed led to lying on the bed, which led to falling asleep and waking not rested and unable to sleep at night.

Food and water was getting low, the chamber pot was full, and the wood was getting low. It was then she heard a click at the door. It opened, Collin entered.

"There's food and water in the back of the wagon. I want you to bring it in."

It felt good to walk out in the open air.

"Oh, and Beth," Collin said as she walked from the cabin. "Don't get any ideas," he concluded with his hand grasping the handle of his revolver.

He kept a close eye on her, as she emptied her chamber pot far from the cabin. Then he allowed her to make a stockpile of wood for the stove.

Back in the cabin, Beth felt determined to speak with Collin about the way she was being treated. Before she could say a word, he pushed her down onto the bed, collapsing on top of her.

"Collin, not in my condition…"

He pressed down harder on her, burying his face in her neck. "Don't be silly. It'll be months before you can't."

She could have argued the point. She could have tried to fight him off. So many alternatives raced through her mind. All of them would be fruitless; he was stronger and had a gun. If she went against him, the best she could hope for was a thrashing. He could easily kill her as killing an insect, which by the way would eliminate all of his problems. No, it was best to hid in that small space in the back of her mind, and not say a word.

When he'd finished, after adjusting his clothing, Collin started towards the door. Putting her fears aside, Beth felt she had to say something.

"Why, Collin, why?" she asked. He turned to look at her. She continued, "Why does it have to be this way?"

A smirk came over his face, just a hint of a smile, only a breath away from laughter.

"You're spoiled, you truly are," he said. "You've forgot who you are. Don't forget you are a slave, my slave. I can do whatever I want with you. It's the law."

"Man's law," she shouted, "not God's law!"

Now, Collin was laughing. "I am your God!" he shouted.

After the door slammed, she heard the click of the padlock.

****

Everyone living on this earth or who has ever lived or will every live understands loneliness. We know what it feels like, its cause and cure. Like a disease it should be avoided, and like a disease, if not treated it will develop into something far worse.

The lack of human contact can turn deadly. Without human contact, no ear to listen, no voice heard, no hand to touch, the person empties of them self and wither away like a tree losing its leaves during a drought.

Beth was in that place. Minutes became hours and hours became days. She started to question her sanity.

Collin's visits, though necessary for survival, did little to ease the pain. If anything it made things worse. For there was no conversation, there was no human contact in the truest sense. Like picking at a wound it delays the healing and makes it worse.

There was one and only one saving grace keeping Beth alive and close to sanity. Her child budding within her, everyday her belly grew larger. She could feel the life inside her, the child moving within her, sometimes even kicking. She'd spend hours with her hands on her stomach, feeling the movement. So close, only inches apart, yet a world away.

Late at night, in bed, the glow from the stove being the only light, she'd rub her stomach. The child would react to her touch. She'd talk to the child ever so gently, sometimes she'd even sing. This was the human touch she needed. This is what kept her sane.

****

It was late autumn, the days were getting longer, and winter was setting in. Beth began showing large, it would not be long. Collin's visits became more frequent. For whatever reason, he stopped having his way with her. This was a blessing.

Winter came, as did the snow. Beth was burning huge amounts of wood to keep warm. Thankfully, Collin always made sure she had enough wood.

Though she had no way of knowing for sure, from the looks of the outside world, she ventured it was December. Perhaps, it would be a Christmas baby?

It was the coldest day yet when Collin arrived, except this time he was not alone. Hearing the wheels of the wagon crunching the snow, Beth hurried to the window. She watched Collin coming up the walk, behind him was an elderly white woman.

Collin unlocked the door and entered with the woman close behind him.

"This is Miriam; she's going to help you have the baby."

Beth only imaged what would happen when the baby arrived. She had no idea of what to do. So, in a way, having a midwife was a comfort. What was not reassuring was the look of Miriam. To say she was elderly was an understatement. The woman looked ancient. She was short, frail, and horribly bent over. Her white hair was unkempt - the likeness of dry straw. Her face embroidered with lines, a hawk nose that hung nearly to her upper lip. The pupils of her eyes were covered over with muskiness, the color of yellowing milk gone sour.

One hundred years ago, they accused women that looked like her of being witches and burned them at the stake.

"Get down flat on the bed," Miriam ordered.

Beth hesitated mostly out of confusion. It was all happening too fast. For some reason unknown to her, she looked to Collin for a sign. The look on his face was one of demanding with no sympathy.

Beth lay flat on the bed, her hands at her side, her eyes staring blankly at the ceiling. Miriam sat on the edge of the bed, placing her hands on Beth's stomach. She felt around till satisfied the child was in the right position.

"Bring your knees up," Miriam said, and then raising Beth's skirt.

Never had Beth been examined down there by a doctor or anyone else, for that matter, and with Collin standing off to the side, it was the most uncomfortable she'd ever felt.

"Any day now," Miriam announced.

"Is it a boy or a girl?" Beth asked.

Miriam broke out laughing, revealing her clean white teeth – all three of them. "You are an ignorant girl."

Miriam continued her inspection as Collin put away the supplies and stoked the fire.

As she stood up, Miriam placed Beth's skirt in order. "Listen to me carefully. I want you to stay in bed as much as possible. I live not too far from here. I'll come by and check on you twice each day. Don't fret; mostly never do babies come in a blink. They usually announce themselves hours before. I'll help you when the time comes."

As they left, Beth looked up in time to see Collin hand Miriam the key. The door slammed closed, and the lock clicked.

****

Beth's plan was simple. Miriam was a frail old woman; when she came to check on her, Beth would overpower her and escape. She held no intentions of hurting the woman, a simple shove out of the way would suffice. However, on the first day Miriam appeared, Beth's plans were dashed.

When she heard the key in the lock, Beth rose, standing at the side of her bed. Miriam opened the door and entered. Beth could easily rush the woman, push her aside and make a run for it. Although, that would surely harm her, Beth decided to wait for Miriam to approach her, and then she would push her down onto the bed. By the time the old woman got to her feet, Beth would be long gone. Surprisingly, Miriam remained in the doorway.

"Before you get any bright ideas, let me explain something," Miriam declared. "You need to understand how lucky you really are. You're only this close from being killed. One bullet to your head and all Mr. Townsend's worries would be over, yet he keeps you alive. Remember that. Before I came today, Mr. Townsend offered me a pistol. I told him I wouldn't need it, because a smart girl like you knows better. You could easily overpower me, but where would you go? Snow's everywhere, it's freezing cold, and you're hours from havin' your baby. Let's say you do get away, and you don't freeze to death, where could you go? Anyone who takes you in, be it friends or family will be put to death. So, for the sake of everybody, including yourself and the life of your baby, do just what you're told."

It was a short and to the point speech that found its mark. All thoughts of escape left Beth's mind.

Miriam did her usual examination. When she finished, she rose from off the edge of the bed, heading for the door.

"Well…?" Beth called to her.

"Well, what?"

"What about my baby?"

"Oh, everything's fine. I don't suspect you'll have it today, surely tomorrow, though. Don't worry; I'll be back in time." Miriam turned her head this way and that, inhaling deeply. "It stinks in here. When was the last time you emptied your chamber pot?"

"Not since you were last here," replied Beth.

"Well, here's your chance. Go empty it. Now…!" shouted Miriam.

Beth reached under the bed, took the pot, and carried it out the door. She walked a few feet from the cabin and emptied it. Walking back to the cabin, Beth realized what Miriam was up to. Just the short walk from the cabin and back, wearing no coat and poor footwear, Beth understood she'd never survive more than an hour traipsing through the snow.

Before closing the door, Miriam made one more announcement. "I suspect you'll have your baby tomorrow. I'll be here early. I'm goin' to ask Mr. Townsend to be here, too. Now, you get plenty of rest, you're goin' to need it."

10

Gone

True to her word, Miriam returned early the next day, and in keeping with her prophecy, Beth began the process, the birth pains started early that day.

The harshness of the pains frightened Beth. She'd heard giving birth was excruciating, only that was hearsay, this was real. She knew about the pangs getting worse, longer, and more often, she knew that much. That was exactly what happened. By midafternoon, the hurt came like waves crashing on a rocky shore.

Surprisingly, Miriam was a great comfort. Her expertise gave Beth a feeling of security and hope that all would turn out well.

Late afternoon, Collin appeared. Standing over the bed, he eyed down at Beth wriggling in pain and moaning. Like Beth, he knew of such things only through word of mouth. His face told it all. He wasn't ready for any of this.

"So, what would you have me do?" he asked Miriam.

She pointed across to a sack near the stove. "I brought some old rags and towels. I want you to tear them into strips." Then she pointed to the water barrel. "Take one of the larger pots; make me some boiling water."

Without a word, he went about his duties. By now, Beth was becoming more aware of what was happening within and to her body, and less aware of what was happening around her.

Before any of them realized the time, darkness was all around. Collin kept the fire going in the stove, not only for its warmth, with the grating open the flames illuminated the room. The wick on the kerosene lamp was at its fullest.

"Take a seat," Miriam told Collin who hovered over the bed like an annoying mosquito. "It's goin' to be a long night."

Again, true to her word, they went on late into the night, past midnight. Beth felt exhausted. She couldn't think straight or hear anything other than her own moans nor could she see anything clearly beyond her nose. Everything was unreal and faraway. Only the pain was real.

The last thing Beth remembered before she lost consciousness was Miriam saying, "Something's wrong."

****

When she woke, the room was flooded with sunlight; it was a new day. The world was nothing more than a blur to Beth. She lay in bed, completely drained, unable to speak or move. All she was aware of was the pain was gone and the sound of a baby crying in the distance echoing over and over.

She heard Miriam and Collin speaking over her.

"She's lost much blood. I can't say if she's going to make it or not. It's out of my hands. All you can do is let her sleep. I'm goin' home," said Miriam.

"You can't leave me like this! Do something!" Collin demanded.

"I just told you there's nothin' I can do. She dies or lives it's none my business."

"What about the other thing?" Collin whispered, as if in fear someone might listen in. "I don't want to do it. You do it. I'll pay you extra."

"Not my worry," replied Miriam. "Now, give me my money, and I'll be on my way."

"Very well," Collin grumbled.

Unable to see, move, or speak, what happened next Beth could only deduce by what she heard. There was a loud wallop sound followed by and even louder thump to the floor. She heard a limp body being dragged out the door, and then the door slamming.

As Collin was a well-built young man and Miriam a frail old woman, Beth came to only one conclusion. Collin struck Miriam, killed her, and lugged her out of the cabin, probably to bury the body.

The cry of a baby, her baby, was all around, as again, she lost consciousness.

****

Her eyes fluttered for a moment, and then opened wide. It took a moment to gain focus. She still felt weak, yet she was able to raise her head. It was daytime that much she knew. She was alone, the cabin was dead silent. Her first thought was of her child.

Using all her strength, she sat up in bed.

"Hello...?" she murmured. A foolish gesture as it was clear no one was there.

She tried to get out of bed, only to fall back down, exhausted.

The lock clicked, and in walked Collin.

"You're awake, good. How do you feel?" he asked, placing a sack of groceries on the table.

For Beth, this was not a time for chitchat. "Where's my child?"

Collin went about the cabin, as if he hadn't heard a word. "Believe it or not, you've been out of it for three days. You lost a lot of blood, wasn't sure you were going to make it."

Beth repeated her question, this time louder and firmer. "Where is my baby?"

Collin stopped his movements, and looked at her squarely. "Oh, that thing, it's gone."

"What do you mean, 'gone'?"

"I sold it to another plantation," he said matter-of-factly with no emotion whatsoever. The soup is hot. The soup is cold. I sold it.

"What plantation?" Beth shouted.

"It's far away, someplace where you'll never find it."

"Why would you do such a thing?"

Collin walked to the side of the bed, smiling down at her. "I've spoiled you. I see that now. You are mine to do with whatever I want. As soon as you said you were pregnant, I could have had you killed. But I didn't. I let you have the baby. Now, it's time to get back to the way things were. With my aunt gone, we can sleep in the same room. Life will be good again."

There were knives of hatred shooting from Beth's eyes. Collin continued.

"Listen, you didn't think I was going to have some mulatto brat running around my house, did you? Get it through your head this is the best it's going to be. Rest; tomorrow I'll have some of the men bring you home."

Collin started for the door.

"What was it?" Beth asked softly.

"What are you talking about?" Collin asked, standing in the doorway.

"Was it a boy or a girl?"

"You don't need to know that," said Collin, shaking his head.

Slamming the door shut, the lock clicked into place.

Tears flowed like a river from Beth's eyes. She cried till she could cry no more. Then suddenly, like the snapping of a twig, Beth began to have thoughts…evil thoughts…thoughts of revenge. She'd not say a word. She'd do whatever she was told, bidding her time. And then one day, when he least expects it…

11

Slow and Painful

How do you kill someone? It's an easy question to answer, until you explore the matter in depth. There are three parts to the undertaking: the *Physical*, the *Preventive* and the *Emotional*.

Physical: Better put…the method of murder. Murder is the purposeful destruction of another human being, hand-to-hand combat, use of an object, loss of blood, loss of breath. All these techniques take skill and muscle, something Beth lacked. Of course, she might prevail in a physical attack using the element of surprise, the easiest of which would be to kill Collin in his sleep. Except, that is the problem with revenge, Beth wanted Collin to know he was dying, and who killed him and why.

Preventive: This goes without saying. Murder is a crime, punishable by death. Your only hope is to not be suspect, to have a foolproof alibi.

Emotional: This is something most people don't consider when contemplating murder. Understand that when you kill someone you have to keep on living with the memory of what you've done. For some people this is too heavy a burden to bear, and must be deeply considered. Not to mention the moral aspects of your actions.

****

As far as Collin understood the world, he was king. Even his dreams were made true. There were other women in his life besides Beth. Only, none of them were slaves from his or any other plantation. They were all white women that lived in the town. Never were they brought to the Townsend Plantation. Collin would ride into town to visit them, sometimes not returning for days. These were the only times Beth felt at ease.

For Beth was truly Collin's mistress. Her room was next to his. He could visit whenever he wanted, day or night. She was at his beck and call. Although she had full access to anywhere on the plantation, she was forbidden to leave the property. Not that there was any place to go to, if she wanted to leave.

As always, no one befriended her, for fear of Collin. Only Ursula crossed that line, and was Beth's only and dearest friend, as well as a confident. Whenever Collin was away, Beth would sit in the kitchen while Ursula cooked, the two of them talking for hours.

"If anyone sold my child out from under me, I think I'd…I'd…I'd kill him. That's what I'd do," Ursula said one day, to Beth's surprise.

The statement took Beth so unexpectedly and sent her so far aback she was unable to speak or look at Ursula.

After a few stirs to a pot of beans, Ursula turned to see Beth seated at the table, a blank stare on her face and a faraway look in her eye. At that moment, Ursula understood what was brewing in Beth's mind.

"So, that's what you're up to!" Ursula said, taking a seat next to Beth.

"What are you saying?" Beth asked.

"I can see it in your eyes," exclaimed Ursula. "When I said I'd kill anyone that took my child away, everything about you changed. That is what you want to do, isn't it? You're going to kill Master Collin, aren't you?"

Beth took her time in answering. She blinked, turned her head, staring directly into Ursula's eyes, she confessed.

"Yes, I want him dead."

A smile glowed on Ursula's face. "You got more guts than brains, but I gotta say I don't blame you. What's takin' you so long?"

"I'm not sure about the where, when, and how. What would you do?"

Ursula laughed, "I'd wait for when he was asleep, and then I'd take a hammer to his head."

"No," Beth snapped. "I want him wide awake and fully aware of what's happening. I want him to suffer."

"My…my…my, you do have it bad, don't you?" commented Ursula. She leaned back in her chair. "Well, let me think about this for a minute." Ursula fixed her eyes on the ceiling, lost in thought. She sat up straight and leaned forward. "I got it. You know what I'd do? Being a cook, I'd poison him. And as he died, rolling in pain, I'd be laughing in his face."

It was then Beth realized she wasn't the only one with hatred in their heart for Collin. "Will you help me?" Beth asked.

Ursula rose from her chair to stir the pot of beans. "It would be my pleasure."

****

What is the difference between a plantation and a farm? There are many, although there is one that is most outstanding. A plantation is a self-sustaining community. The people who work the land (mostly slaves) live on the property. Most of their needs they take care of themselves, especially food. There is little need for the outside world. However, there are some supplies even they can't provide. For this reason, every week or so, Ursula rode a wagon into town, buying what was needed at the General Store.

For little more than a week, Master Collin stayed away. It would be a good guess to say he'd return soon. Ursula took the wagon to get the supplies needed to keep him well feed in the manner he was use to.

McCullers' General Store would have everything she needed. The payment for the supplies Collin paid monthly. She was never questioned about her purchases, until that day.

"Arsenic…! What you be needing that for?" Mr. McCullers asked, holding up the can, inspecting the label.

"Got a mess of varmints: rats, snakes, raccoons, you name it, we got 'em," answered Ursula.

"Well, you be careful with this stuff," McCullers warned. "It ain't got no color or taste. If you want to be on the safe side, I'd buy some cocoa powder and color it brown or something so nobody gets poisoned. Besides, the cocoa gives it a taste. Varmints love sweet."

"That's a good idea, Mr. McCullers," responded Ursula. "I'll take a can of cocoa powder. It's always best to be on the safe side."

****

On the way back to the Townsend Plantation, Ursula was stopped by Master Collin on the road. He was on horseback, riding home.

"Master Collin, I figured you'd be coming home today, so I went to McCullers' to get you something nice for dinner."

Collin looked at the supplies in the back of the wagon. "Very good, I can hardly wait. I'll be up in my room resting. Call me when dinner's ready."

"Yes, Master Collin."

With that, Collin galloped on ahead.

Beth helped Ursula bring the supplies into the kitchen. Normally, Collin could be demanding of Beth when he rested in the afternoon. She was grateful to whomever it was Collin spent the week with, she'd taken the wind out of his sails.

"Is this is…?" Beth questioned, holding a can.

"No, that's cocoa powder. The grocer suggested I put some in with the arsenic, so I don't confuse it with anything else, especially wheat flour. It looks a lot like it." Ursula held another can up to Beth. "This is it."

"How are you going to do it?" Beth asked.

"Like I said, it looks a lot like wheat flour. And that's exactly how I'm going to use it. First, I'm going to bake some bread. I'll mix a little of it in with the flour. I'm also going to make stew for tonight, some meat and plenty of vegetables. I always thicken it with flour. I'm goin' to this time, too, only with some arsenic thrown in.

"Before I thicken it, I'm gonna put some stew aside for you. So, if Master Collin wants you to sup with him, I'll make sure you get the stew without the poison. Just be sure you don't eat no bread."

Beth inspected the can. "You sure this is going to be enough?"

Ursula laughed. "Don't you worry none, it only takes a little bit, and I'm gonna give him a whole lot. It won't be quick either. He's gonna be rolling in pain for the last few hours of his life. You'll have plenty of time to give him what for."

****

They sat at the dining room table, Collin at the head, Beth at his side. Neither one spoke, communication stopped a long time ago for the two of them. Thankfully, his demands on Beth were less frequent. Recently, he started going into town to satisfy his passions more and more. It was clear, Collin was tiring of her. If this was a good thing or a bad thing, Beth wasn't sure. It was a blessing to not be pestered by him. Yet, if he truly and fully tired of her what would he do about her? If he wanted her gone, it was up to his discretion when and how it would be done.

The wine was poured, a glass to their right, water glass to their left, cutlery to the left and right. Ursula came from the kitchen and placed bread and butter before them. Returning to the kitchen, she came back with two steaming bowls of stew. Placing one before each, she curtsied and then back to the kitchen.

Collin took hold of a piece of bread and buttered it. He dipped his spoon into the bowl. He was about to put the spoonful into his mouth, he turned to see Beth staring at him, her hands at her side.

"My dear, you're not eating," he commented.

"I'm not hungry."

"Well, if you're not going to eat, you might as well go to your room. All the better, I prefer eating alone just now, I'll come to you when I've finished."

Beth rose, walking from the room. Just before climbing the stairs, she stopped and looked back to see Collin still holding the spoonful before him.

"Go ahead, I'll be up in a minute," he called to her.

Beth inhaled, holding her breath, she ascended the staircase. In her room, she lay on her bed, and waited.

"Ursula!" Collin shouted.

The next moment, Ursula dashed from the kitchen and stood by the dining table. "Yes, Master Collin."

Collin reached over, placed a spoon in Beth's bowl of stew. He lifted a spoonful and let it pour back into the bowl. "Look here. This is Beth's stew. Look how watery it is compared to mine." He did the same with his own bowl. The thick brew dripped slowly. "See how thick and rich mine is."

"Where is Beth?" Ursula asked.

"She wasn't hungry so she went up to her room. It doesn't matter," he snapped. "Let's consider the problem at hand. Sit down!" he ordered sternly, pointing to the chair at the opposite end of the table.

Ursula did as she was told. Rising from his chair, Collin took up his bowl, walked to the other end of the table and placed it before her. "Now, taste it!"

"Master Collin, I always eat my dinner in the kitchen."

"I want you to eat it, now!"

"But, Master Collin…"

Collin reached into his jacket, pulling out a derringer, and pointed it at her.

"I said, 'eat!'."

He walked back to the other end of the table, sitting down, continuing to aim the derringer at her.

With shaking hands, she took up the spoon, dipped it in the stew, brought up a morsel and placed it in her mouth.

Collin took a piece of bread and tossed it across the table to her. "Here, have some bread with it."

Taking up the piece of bread, Ursula continued to eat.

"Do you know where I was this past week?" Collin asked. He laughed. "Of course, you don't. I was the guest of Mrs. Cummings. Her husband's away on business. I must say it was a most gratifying time for both of us. She is… how shall I put this? Mrs. Cummings is a most gracious hostess. Regretfully, eventually it was time to leave and come home. Well, figuring I was already in town, I decided to pay my monthly bill at the General Store. Mr. McCullers is a talkative old cuss. He told me you were in just that day to pick up some odds and ends, one of which was some arsenic. I never knew we had a varmint problem? Don't stop eating!"

Collin kept her in his aim, as he rambled on. It took some time; eventfully she finished the entire meal. Again, Collin rose and walked over, and inspected the bowl.

"All gone, good job, Ursula, well done, you've been a good girl. Forget about cleaning up. Take the night off. Why don't you go to your room, and have a rest."

Ursula rose slowly up from her chair. With her head bowed, she walked off to her room.

****

Collin never bothered to knock whenever he entered Beth's room. This time was different. He kicked the door in. Beth shot up from bed to a standing position.

"You need to help your friend. Ursula isn't well. She's deathly sick."

Beth stood in a daze, looking at him.

"She's in her room." He clapped his hands a few times to get her attention. "Quick, run to her!"

Beth dashed passed him and out the room. As she rushed down the stairs, she heard Collin laughing loudly.

Ursula slept in a small room off the kitchen. Entering, Beth expected to find Ursula on her bed. However, she found her on the floor vomiting into her chamber pot.

"Ursula!" shouted Beth as she fell to her knees.

"Help me up; get me on the bed." It was an effort just to raise her head. "Please, I don't want to die on the floor."

"You're not going to die," Beth replied, still struggling to get Ursula on the bed.

"Of course, I'm goin' to die," Ursula shouted in a half laugh, half cry.

Finally, Beth plopped her down on the bed.

"What can I do?" Beth asked.

"Water, get me some water! I'm so thirsty!"

Beth rushed into the kitchen, returning with a mug filled with water. Ursula put it to her lips and tilted her head back, spilling most of it. She tensed for a moment, dropping the mug. Her body stiffened; she began moaning and finally screaming in pain.

She grabbed Beth's hand tightly. "Don't leave me! I don't want to die alone!"

"I'm here. Don't worry, I'm here."

For nearly an hour, Beth sat on the edge of the bed, holding the poor woman's hand, listening to her groan in pain. Ursula took in a deep breath, let it out slowly, and all was calm. Beth knew she was dead. Dying may be painful, however, death is painless.

****

Without knocking, Beth crashed into Collin's bedroom. She found him primping in front of a full-length mirror.

"She's dead," Beth announced.

He turned from his mirror to look at her. "Dead, you say. That's too bad. She was a good cook. It must have been something she ate," he said, exploding into laughter. He continued, "You know, if I ever find out you had anything to do with this, you'll meet the same fate."

A fire burned in Beth's heart; still, she was determined to remain calm.

"Why am I here, Collin?"

"You're here because I own you; you're my property. You are, for lack of a better word, my mistress."

"That may be true," admitted Beth. "Nevertheless, you have increasingly lost interest in me. Why else would you spend so much time with the women in town? And now you have suspicions I might be trying to kill you. If you have any business sense, you'd sell me."

"I could always send you to work in the fields, here. Better yet, I could just have you killed," he replied.

"You owe me, Collin!" she shouted, not a hint of fear in her voice. "You took my child away and sold it! You owe me, Collin!" Taking a deep breath, she returned to calmness. "If you feel anything for me, Collin, if you've ever felt anything for me, please, sell me."

He took a long moment to answer, and he pointed to the door. "Waste not, want not, I always say. Very well, go to your room and pack your things. I'm selling you. You leave in the morning."

12

The Tanner Plantation

The Tanner Plantation was only a few miles from the Townsend property. One of Collin's men drove the carriage taking Beth to the sale. Collin wasn't present; lawyers carried out the transaction.

The Tanner Plantation was like any other plantation in the county with one factor that separated it from all the others: the owners, Mr. and Mrs. Tanner.

Wilhelm Tanner and his wife, Anna, emigrated from Switzerland when they were young newlyweds. They came to America with family and friends seeking a new and better life. They settled in Pennsylvania to work the mines, save for Wilhelm and Anna. Wilhelm's ambition was to work the land.

After working for others, throughout many states, always learning and saving their money, the Tanners bought a small farm in Mississippi. After years of hard work, struggling, and saving, they expanded their domain by buying smaller farms connected to theirs. In time, their spread was over six hundred acres.

A man of good judgment and business, Wilhelm understood the future was cotton. They converted from a farm to a plantation. Within ten years, they were one of the most profitable cotton plantations in the county.

The Tanner's success story was no different from many others. What did make the Tanners stand out from all their other neighbors was they were Mennonites. This affected their dress, their speech, their way of life, and their way of thinking and dealing with the world.

The Bible was their guide to everything they did in their lives, although, there were many who would disagree with their interpretations. Being the only Mennonites in the county, perhaps the entire state, they made do with becoming members of the local church.

What made them stand out from others was their physical appearance, being what most folk would call Amish in style. Wilhelm always dressed in black, pants, jacket, wide brim hat, and a bright white shirt. His long graying beard, minus a mustache, touched his chest.

His wife, Anna, dressed modestly to excess. Her dresses were always long sleeved to her wrists where they met the cuffs of her gloves, which she always wore. The necklines of her dresses were just that, it rose halfway up her neck. As well, she constantly wore a bonnet that covered her entire head, and framed her face with stiff white linen. Rumor was she even wore this covering to bed.

The life of a slave was just as hard as it was at any other plantation, except for one particularity. Being Mennonites, the Tanners believed in nonviolence; although, this needs study in detail. This meant no killings, no hangings or gunshots to the head. Still, it did not stop sever whippings, cutting off limbs, and other forms of torture.

****

"Mr. Townsend advised us to use you as a housemaid. He says you're very good at such work," said Mrs. Tanner coldly, her mouth such a fine straight line, so tight it would crack like marble if she was ever to smile. "However," continued Mrs. Tanner, "If you every slack, it's the fields for you."

Beth nodded agreeing. She would do anything to avoid fieldwork, a much harder way of life, a way of living that shortens your living.

They took Beth to her shack. It was a small one room, run-down structure. No slaves lived in the main house.

She was to report for work on Monday. This was Saturday. All slaves received Sunday off, as it was a day of rest, another perk of working for Mennonites.

Monday morning, Beth was first to arrive; determined to do her best the whole day long.

At the end of the day, she was one of the last to leave. She'd made an impression on Mrs. Tanner, and the old woman told her so.

"Your first day here was more than satisfactory. If you can keep up this momentum, all will be well. You've found yourself a home here at the Tanner Plantation. Remember, God helps those who help themselves."

"Yes, ma'am"

Beth was willing to work hard. Her past had been hell; hopefully, this would be better.

One especially large difference now in Beth's life was the people around her. No longer the beauty to be sold as a mistress or being a mistress of the master, the world of friendship opened up to her.

Her neighbors knocked on her door to introduce themselves. Her co-workers treated her kindly and with respect. Best of all was the attention she received from eligible young men, although sometimes not so eligible older men. They smiled at her, approached her, asked her name, and made a fuss over her. All in all, life was good, getting better, and full of hope.

Sundays were the best. To sit with her head high without convicting looks and gossiping whispers made going to church a joy. Strange though, never was there a sign of her old friends, Fanny and Dahlia. What was more mysterious was the absence of her father and sister. This was upsetting. She kept her eyes peeled; hoping one Sunday she'd see them.

Attending Church Service was not the only reason Sundays were so special. After church, every slave at the Tanner Plantation rushed home, changed into their comfortable clothes, and there in the slave quarters they'd gather for what can be only described as a community potluck. Everyone brought food and laughter. Musicians gathered, and music filled the air, although, there was no dancing, as Mrs. Tanner forbid such unruliness.

It was always a joyous occasion, like Christmas and New Years blended for a day. As for Beth, it was night and day compared to her life at other plantations. People treated her well. She made friends. And the young men all had an eye for her. It was a good thing dancing wasn't allowed. Beth would need a new pair of dancing shoes every month.

On one particular Sunday afternoon, during the gathering, young men surrounded Beth, each courting and competing for her attention. She smiled and remained polite, yet still aloof.

From the corner of her eye she saw three young men walking passed. She felt sure she'd never seen them before. They seemed as disinterested in her and her in them. They walked in a straight line, one behind the other.

When the first young man walked by, he turned, looking directly at her. There was sternness in his glance, a demanding man with a strength that made him able to give orders, yet a defiance that made him not take them.

When the second young man passed, he too looked straight at her. It was then she realized his resemblance to the first man. However, there was a softness to him the first man could never posses. The second man's glance was not half as intense as the first, a passive man, a follower and not a leader, and not caring who knew it.

She then noticed the built and stride of the third man. She understood these three were brothers, each with slight and major differences, but clearly from the same tree.

The saying goes, *Lightning never strikes twice*. For Beth this wasn't so. As soon as her eyes met with the eyes of the third young man, she knew him. The world stopped for a moment and started the process of change.

It was the same young man she'd seen at the wedding of Jojoba and Nelly at the Colby Plantation so long ago. The silent bond they formed that day was now renewed. From the look on both their faces, each knew the other and what they thought.

He stopped following his brothers and started towards her.

As if in a trance, she broke out of the circle of admirers and met him halfway. All the suitors she left behind stood speechless, looking at one another in bewilderment.

"I never thought I'd ever see you again," she whispered.

"I always knew we'd see each other again," he responded with a smile.

She smiled back.

"What's your name?"

"Beth."

"I'm Gray. It's great to finally meet you," he said, offering his hand in friendship, which felt strange. Both of them experienced a strong urge to lean forward and kiss. "I thought you were at the Colby Plantation?"

"I was…"

"Then how did you wind up here?"

"It's long story."

"Good, that means when I ask to hear it I'll be with you for a long time. That sounds wonderful."

She looked down, feeling a mixture of shyness and young girl glee.

"Let's go for a walk. So, we can talk. Follow me, I know just the place."

She would have followed him anywhere. They walked along the edge of the fields where they could be alone. There was an interesting chemistry between them, a feeling of knowing each other not only well but for a long time. Of course this wasn't true, yet they couldn't deny that was what it felt like.

Gray was born and bred on the Tanner Plantation. He knew no other life than this one, having never been more than five miles from where he was born. He was the youngest of three brothers, Victor, the oldest, James in the middle, and he the baby. He was one year older than Beth.

Their parents died not too many years ago. It was a rough time for the three young men, still with love and respect they survived. They lived together in a small shack not much bigger than the one Beth lived in. They were a family of three, working together, living together, and caring for one another. Other than that, his life story was simple and quick to tell.

After hearing Gray's uncomplicated story, a feeling came over Beth, one of shame and confusion. This was the time for honesty, yet she couldn't bring herself to be so. Not that she lied. She told him about living on the Colby Plantation, the death of her mother, living with her father and sister. However, she never spoke about General Colby's plans to sell her off as a mistress, or how she ruined it all with a wagon accident. She only told him she'd been sold to the Townsend Plantation, and then to the Tanner Plantation. She omitted any word about Master Collin, about being his mistress, having his baby, and having the child sold out from under her. As far as Gray was concerned, Beth was just this unbelievingly beautiful woman with a simple past behind her, and hopefully with him in her future.

13

Amends

The entire plantation took for granted and respected the courtship of Beth and Gray. Although, many a young woman eyed Gray, and young men Beth, still, all relations were nothing more than friendships. Everyone believed this would take root, grow, and one day blossom into marriage. Beth and Gray felt the same.

Every Sunday, she and Gray would spend the morning at church service, sitting in the front pew, alongside his two brothers. As for Victor and James, they were always cordial to Beth; although, never too friendly or excited about the relationship. Being older, they remained neutral about it all. They watched over their younger brother like two mother hens. For them, only time would tell.

It was on one particular Sunday service, as they all stood singing hymns; Beth looked across the aisle to see her sister, Louise. She nearly didn't recognize her; Louise grew into a mature looking young woman, as pretty as Beth. What caught Beth's attention, giving her a cause for worry, was that their father was not beside her, she was alone.

Beth and Louise smiled at each other across the aisle. Through hand signals and eye contact, they each understood they would talk after service.

Anticipation consumed Beth. She couldn't concentrate on the sermon; her mind occupied. Noticing the change in her, Gray placed his hand on hers, reached over and whispered in her ear.

"Are you all right?"

"I'm fine. I'll tell you later," she whispered back.

The moment the service ended, Beth and Louise rushed across the aisle into each other's arms.

"I've been looking for you for weeks," Beth said. "Where have you been?"

"I couldn't get away. It's Papa, he's not well. He's dying. I came today in hopes I'd see you."

Just then Gray and his brothers came on them. Beth turned, and made the introduction. "Oh, everyone, this is my little sister, Louise." Then Beth smiled. "Although, she doesn't look little anymore, you've grown so much since I last saw you." Beth pointed to Gray and then his brothers. "Louise, this is my betrothed, Gray, and his brothers Victor and James."

It was a slip of the tongue. Why she referred to Gray as her betrothed was a mystery even to her. Interesting to note, the term didn't surprise Gray or catch him off guard. Where as Victor raised an eyebrow in surprise and James looked stunned and neither of them showed any sign of being pleased.

"It's my father, he's not well," Beth whispered to Gray. "I need to go to him."

"I'll go with you," Gray offered.

"No, you go on with your brothers. I won't be long. I promise."

"You're sure."

"I'll be fine."

****

Entering the old familiar shack, Beth looked to her father's bed. At first, she thought it was empty, until she saw him stir. He'd lost so much weight; he barely made a dent in the bed.

Louise reached out, placing her hand on his shoulder, shaking him gently. "Wake up, Papa. Look who's here to see you. It's Beth."

"Beth?" He murmured, pulling the blanket away. He tried to sit up, only to fall back down onto the mattress.

"Try not to move, Papa," Louise said softly. She leaned toward Beth and whispered, "Don't let him talk too much. He has so little strength left."

Beth sat on the edge of the bed, reaching out, stroking the side of his face, assuring him she was there. He opened his eyes to look at her; a small weak smile appeared on his lips.

"Beth!"

She scarcely recognized him. His eyes and cheeks were sunken. His entire body was no more than a skeleton covered with loose fitting skin.

Louise handed a cup of warm broth to Beth. "See if you can get him to eat some. He hasn't eaten in days."

When she put the cup to his lips, he found the strength to gently push her hand away.

"It doesn't matter, anymore," he said. "It's all right, everything's in place, now that you're here. I can die in peace."

"What are you talking about, Papa; you're going to be just fine."

He let out a small puff of breath, similar to a laugh. "I may not have been a good father, but I never taught you to lie. Of course, I'm going to die…tonight."

Beth sat, holding his hand as he slept.

****

The room slowly emptied of all light. Night approached, slipping through the cracks in the walls, filling up the room. Beth was still holding her father's hand; Louise sat in a chair, looking on. Gradually, Old Tom's eyes opened. The rest did him good; he seemed more alert.

"All those years I drank like a fish. People would say, 'Old Tom, you better stop your drinkin'. You're gonna drink yourself to death. So, what happens? I drink for years with not so much as chipping a nail. I stop drinking and the chariots come to carry me home."

"You rest, Papa," Louise warned.

"There'll be time enough for rest, tomorrow," he replied.

Both girls knew what he meant, by morning he'd be gone. They went silent, letting him speak.

"I want to say how sorry I am to both of you girls. I don't know. When your momma died, I lost it for a while. I couldn't stand losing her. I was mad at God for takin' her. I was angry that I still had you two. I wanted to die; only, I didn't have the courage to put a bullet to my head, and get it over with. So, I decided to commit suicide in the slowest way possible. I started in to drinkin'. Funny thing is, I never even liked the taste of the stuff. But it did stop the pain, for a while. When your momma died, she left a hole in my heart. I tried to fill it with moonshine when what I really needed was sunshine. I found the Lord late in life. Like they say, 'Better late than never'. Now that I'm willin' to be a good father, He's taken me away. Forgive me girls."

"You were a good father," Louise claimed.

Old Tom snickered. "That's two lies in one night. Pretty soon you'll be catching up to the Apostle Peter. No, just say you forgive me, and I can die in peace."

"We forgive you, Papa," Beth said, taking hold of his hand.

Louise sat on the opposite edge of the bed and took his other hand.

A tiny smile of contentment appeared on his face, he closed his eyes, went unconscious and silent, breathing short shallow breaths.

With each passing hour, his breathing became more labored. Not being able to swallow, there was a gurgling sound in his throat and lungs.

They never so much as lit a candle, sitting in the dark, holding their father's hands. Finally, the morning sunlight oozed like honey through the windows, turning the room to gold.

His breathing stopped, and after a long suspenseful minute, started again. This happened over and over for nearly ten minutes. Then without warning, he stopped breathing, and never started again.

Beth and Louise remained sitting, holding his hands. The sound of birds outside flying overhead mingled with the sound of the wind. Suddenly, a knock at the door shattered the peace.

****

Louise's eyes filled with suspicion and fear. She let go of her father's hand and walked to open the door. After all she'd been through, her mind wasn't thinking clearly; she didn't recognize the young man.

"Yes, may I help you?" she asked.

"Is Beth here?"

Beth knew the voice, immediately. "Gray!" she exclaimed, rushing to the door. "Gray, what are you doing here?"

"Beth, you've been away all night. You need to come back with me this instant, before they know you're missing."

"Papa's gone," Beth said solemnly.

Gray was truly sympathetic; still there was concern in his voice. "I'm sorry about your father, Beth, but you need to come back now."

Louise took hold of her sister by the arm. "He's right. You need to go. Don't worry; I'll take care of everything here." Beth remained motionless, as if lost in thought. "Go!" Louise shouted, finally getting through to her sister.

Gray took hold of Beth, taking her by the hand and literally pulling her along.

There was a horse waiting at the outer fence of the Colby Plantation. Gray took it without permission and in too much of a hurry to saddle the beast. It took a minute for both of them to mount, and then they were off.

The moment they rode onto the Tanner property, a group of overseers stopped them. In the outside world this was the equivalent of being arrested.

The charges were abandonment of their posts and horse theft. The entire slave population of the Tanner Plantation was forced to gather in front of the main house. It wasn't to be a court, per say, it was Mr. and Mrs. Tanner passing judgment and handing down punishment. The Tanners considered themselves to be fair-minded, though not always right, it was better than most other plantations.

Mr. and Mrs. Tanner stood on the porch, Beth and Gray at the foot of the steps, all others gathered around as close as possible. Mr. Tanner stepped forward.

"You are accused of running off and robbery of one of my horses."

Gray wanted so much to speak, except he knew it wasn't allowed. Thankfully, Mr. Tanner was a man with an open inquisitive mind.

"Then again, to accuse you of these crimes is inconsistent with your actions. A runaway does not come back and a horse thief does not return the horse. So, I will be lenient. Still, rules are important for our existence, and rules have been broken. Wrong doing bring with it a penalty that must be paid.

"Instead of the usual whipping, we will use a switch. Both of you will receive one dozen lashes with a switch no thicker than my thumb."

Mrs. Tanner stepped forward. Taking hold of her husband by the arm, she whispered into his ear.

"My wife tells me that these two are engaged to be married, asking me to be even more merciful. So be it. It will only be a half dozen lashes each."

"Sir, please, may I speak?" Gray called out.

Everyone went silent. They all understood this was something never done, and might worsen the matter. To everyone's surprise, Mr. Tanner was open to hearing what Gray had to say.

"You may speak."

"Mr. Tanner, sir, I know you to be a fair and honest man, as wise a man as King Solomon. True, we have committed infractions and restitution must be paid. Only, I ask you…no, I plead with you, let the punishment fall on me, alone. I will receive the dozen lashes in payment for the wrongs committed."

Mr. Tanner stood silently thinking. Again, his wife whispered in his ear. He considered what she said and what was in his heart and mind.

"Very well, so be it. You will carry the brunt of the punishment."

"No!" shouted Beth, rushing to Gray, grabbing hold of him, burying her face into his chest, crying. "No, I won't let you do this."

"It's all right, Beth. It's best this way."

He tried to push her away, yet she would not let go of him, clinging to him with all her might. The next moment she felt strong hands pulling her from him.

"Leave me alone. Don't touch me!" she cried.

The hands were too strong for her to resist. She lost her grip on Gray, and taken away to stand with the rest of the crowd. Turning, she realized it was Gray's brothers, Victor and James, holding her back.

"Why are you doing this? Let go of me!" she insisted.

Victor, the oldest and strongest of the brothers, took hold of her by her arms and shook her until she calmed and went silent.

"Listen to me," he demanded. "You want Gray to be your man, well then, let him be that man. Stand by him in his decision. Don't make it any harder for him than it is."

She went quiet, standing and watching with the others, Victor and James at her side.

The overseers were firm yet respectful. They gave Gray enough time to remove his shirt. Unable to face the crowd, he kept his back to them. Two overseers held him by his wrists, holding him in place. The largest of the overseers, a mountain of a man, stepped forward, holding a long switch taken from a bush. He'd removed the leaves making it slick as a razor.

The entire slave population moaned when the first lash cut into Gray's skin. The sound was a whoosh and then a loud crack. Gray's body stiffened with pain; however, he didn't as much as whimper. Again and again he received the lashing in silence, his back dripping with blood. He would be scarred for life.

After the dozen lashes, the overseers let go of him. He fell to the ground like a stone, lying motionless. His two brothers rushed to his side and lifted him to his feet. Beth ran to them, picking up Gray's shirt. Victor took the shirt from Beth and spoke to her sternly.

"If you love my brother, tell him so, and then leave. Go to your own home. Let us take care of him. Let him have his pride."

Beth rushed to stand before Gray. "Darling, I love you," and she kissed him. He could only answer in a moan. She watched as his brothers guided him off. Mr. and Mrs. Tanner went back into their house. The crowd scattered. With tears in her eyes, Beth found her way back to her home.

17

The Wedding

Gray was up and about the next day, yet it wasn't till the following week he recovered from his lashing. Taking Victor's advice, Beth showed concern for Gray's mishap, although after bringing the subject up when she first saw him, she never mentioned it again. Life skipped a beat and was now once more on course, for the time being.

Young love can be so exciting, so full of hope. The seed Beth and Gray planted took root and was now slowly blossoming. Soon, it would bear fruit.

It was on a Sunday after church service while everyone gathered for their weekly picnic in the slave quarters Beth and Gray went for their walk.

When they'd passed the fields of cotton and were at the foot of the forest, Gray stopped. Taking hold of Beth, he drew her to him and kissed her long and hard. Then he backed away a tad, still holding on to her, he stared into her eyes.

To her surprise, never taking his eyes off her, he fell down on one knee.

"I've never known truelove until now. Make me the happiest man in the world, Beth. Marry me!"

She smiled at him, answering without hesitation. "Yes, of course I will."

He rose to his feet and kissed her.

"Oh, I can hardly wait," he whispered in her ear.

As they walked along, hand in hand, they excitedly began making plans.

"We can have a June wedding," Beth said with excitement.

Gray stopped in his tracks. "June? That's a long way off. I was thinking more like next week."

"Next week!" she laughed. "That won't give me much time."

He spoke with all seriousness. "Beth, I have no question in my mind that you are the one for me. We've courted for a time, and I think you're everything I could ever want in a woman. In all that time, I've shown nothing but respect for you, have I not?"

"Yes, that's true," she agreed.

"I've held you in my arms and kissed you, and never have I gone any further than that. I have to tell you I've been tempted; however, I've always held back out of high esteem for you, and because I think of what we have as sacred."

"That's true. You've always been and are a gentleman."

"To be honest, I don't think I can hold out any longer. Yes, I want you as my spouse, I want you in my life, and as much as that, I want you in my bed. The temptation is becoming too great. God forgive me. I have to confess, there's a part of me that wants you here and now. Even Saint Paul said: *If they cannot contain, let them marry: for it is better than to burn.* And my dear Beth, I burn for you. If you love me, marry me. If you love me, marry me, soon. I say a week's time, only because that is my limit. I cannot take it any longer."

Beth smiled; a part of her wanted to laugh, mostly from nervousness. However, she feared he'd take it wrong. So, she contained her nerves, and kept it to a smile. At first, she didn't know what or how to think. Then she realized what she truly felt, and she was not shy to tell him.

"Gray, I love you more than I ever thought I could love. And if I am to be honest, I feel the same way as you. I want to live and die with you, and part of that living is my passion, and it's all for you."

Gray gleamed like the morning sun. If ever the right words were said, it was at that moment.

"Next week?" he asked softly.

"Next week," she said looking shyly at the ground.

****

First rule of being a slave is your life is not your own. Gray asked Mr. and Mrs. Tanner permission to marry. Thankfully, they held no qualms, and when Gray assured them there was no premarital contact, they gave their blessing.

Next was to make arrangements with the church. Reverend Gaines was thrilled. He scheduled the wedding for that Sunday after service. The usual Sunday get-together at the Tanner slave quarters would now be their wedding celebration. Folks were too poor to expect gift giving; instead they planned an elaborate menu.

Gray's brothers gave what they could. The three brothers lived together in one of the larger shacks in the quarter. Since now there would only be the two brothers, Victor and James volunteered to switch homes with Beth. They would move into Beth's smaller home, giving up their home for Beth and Gray. She was in tears when they told her. It was a noble and heart moving gift. They planned to move their things into Beth's home the day of the wedding, so they'd spend their wedding night in their new home.

Victor, being the oldest, would give Beth away. James would be Gray's best man. Although this was fine in Beth's mind, it brought up one extremely difficult problem. Who would be the maid of honor? In her mind, there was only one answer, and that was her sister, Louise. How could they make that happen?

Beth knew even if she could get word to her sister, General Colby would never give his permission for her to attend. He worked his slaves seven days each week. In his mind, giving his people permission to attend church Sunday mornings was enough to get him canonized as a saint.

It was the hand of Mrs. Tanner that changed everything. It was in the afternoon; Beth was doing the wash in an old wooden tub. Mrs. Tanner came outside holding a towel. "Here's one I forgot to give you," she said, handing Beth the limp towel. "So, my dear, how are your wedding arrangements coming?" she asked in a mild tone. It's interesting to note that although when it came to rules and regulations she could be cold and hard as steel. When giving orders she'd spout them like a military sergeant. However, in everyday conversation she was gentle as a lamb and respectful to all.

"It's coming along just fine. I only wish…" Beth stopped midsentence.

"Go ahead, child," Mrs. Tanner said, sounding like a concerned mother. "You only wish…what?"

"That my sister could attend, I'd like her to be my maid of honor. Only, she's at the Colby Plantation. I see my sister every Sunday at church, except we're marrying this Sunday. Still, even if I could get word to her, I'm sure her master would never let her come."

Mrs. Tanner smiled, a rare event, to be sure. "Don't you worry, my dear." The old woman tapped the side of her nose. "I know how to handle General Irwin Colby. Leave it to me."

With that she entered the house, leaving Beth befuddled, yet somehow hopeful.

****

The following day, Beth was changing the bedsheets in the main bedroom. Unexpectedly, Mr. and Mrs. Tanner entered.

"Yes, what do you need?" Beth asked, not sure of what to say.

Mrs. Tanner was not only smiling, she looked downright ecstatic as she approached Beth.

"Your wish has been granted. My husband secured you sister to be with you this Sunday."

Mr. Tanner spoke in a fatherly manner. "General Colby agreed on one condition: that he receives a day's wages for the girl, the day of work he would be missing from her. He demanded one dollar, which is ridiculous. He doesn't even pay his overseers a dollar a day. Don't you fret, I paid him the wage. You may consider it our wedding gift to you."

Beth was nearly in tears. "Oh, Mr. and Mrs. Tanner, thank you. God bless you both."

Mrs. Tanner continued smiling. "We pray that yours is a good and Godly marriage, and that you bear good, strong, and obedient children for us."

Beth continued to force a smile to hide how hurtful those remarks truly were.

****

Sunday, everyone concerned with the wedding was up early. There was so much to do.

Victor and James were up before dawn, transferring Beth's belongings to their home, and their belongings to Beth's home. Gray would have helped them, only there was the chance Beth would be there. Everyone knows it's bad luck for the groom to see the bride before their wedding.

Reverend Gaines spent the night before on his sermon, however, he spent the early morning jotting down Bible verses for the wedding. He was determined to make it a memorable day for the couple.

Louise was so excited she couldn't sleep. She was up before dawn, dressing and primping. She couldn't help thinking of their father; how happy he'd be.

The musicians rehearsed every day, late into the night. The day of the wedding they met to brush up on a few pieces. Everything was to be perfect.

The night before, some of the men slaughtered a large pig, cleaned it, and buried it in a pit with hot coals. They'd dig it up midafternoon, by then it will be fully cooked, juicy and sweet.

Many of the households cooked dozens of side dishes, and of course, there was to be a wedding cake, large enough for all.

Lastly, a group of ladies prepared Beth to look her best for the blessed day. They groomed her, washed and primped her hair, like handmaidens do for their princess in a fairytale.

****

They packed the church to the rafters; everyone dressed in their Sunday finest. They decorated the front of the church with flowers like it was Easter. Wanting to keep the day joyous and light, Pastor Gaines purposely omitted any fire and brimstone from his sermon. He spoke on the *Prodigal Son*, one of everyone's favorites, a story of love and redemption with a happy ending, what could be more fitting?

When service finished, most folks remained in their seats. Pastor Gaines stepped out from behind the podium to stand front and center. Off in the corner, a fiddle player checked his tuning. He spent much of the night rehearsing the wedding march. Gray with his brother, James, as his best man at his side stood to the left of Pastor Gaines. Standing outside at the top of the church steps was Beth's maid of honor, her sister, Louise, looking like the angel she was. And lastly, standing at the front door was Victor, dressed in his finest with Beth on his arm.

Always a breathtaking beauty, Beth was stunning. A glow of loveliness shined within her, touching everyone who looked into her eyes.

"…you nervous?" Victor asked Beth, "Because I am."

Beth couldn't help laughing. It was good to know she was not the only one. "Yeah, me too…"

Both of them had no idea what Gray was going through. He was absolutely panicky.

"Gray…Gray…" James whispered over and over to get his brother's attention. "You're not gonna pass out or anything?"

"What?" Gray answered, completely distracted.

The music was their cue. When the fiddler began, Victor opened the church door. Louise was first to walk down the aisle carrying a small wicker basket filled with red rose peddles. She scattered them down the aisle up to the front of the church where she stood opposite the groom and best man.

Beth clung to Victor's arm as they marched up the aisle. All the people stood smiling; all eyes were on Beth. Coming to the front of the church, Gray stepped forward, smiling from ear to ear.

"Who gives this woman?" Pastor Gaines questioned.

"I do," Victor announced, handing over the bride to the groom.

Holding hands, Beth and Gray stood facing the pastor.

Everyone knew Reverend Gaines as a good preacher. Only, not until they witnessed him perform a wedding did they realize his true talent. Many folk admit they cry at weddings. However, Reverend Gaines could warm the coldest heart of stone. By the end of the ceremony there wasn't a dry eye.

It was heartwarming to see two people so deeply in love. The way they held on to each other, looking into each other's eyes, everyone could feel the love they possessed. When the moment came Reverend Gaines said, "You may now kiss the bride", it was as if the roof of the church flew away. A choir of angels sung aloud, and the hand of God touched every heart in this house of worship.

Beth and Gray turned and walked the aisle to the exit, as folks stood applauding. Outside, the couple stood under a large oak tree, waiting for the crowd. Gray never shook so many hands in his life or received so many pats on his back, or motherly hugs from every old woman in the congregation.

It was the same with Beth, handshakes, hugs, kisses, although, there were one or two kisses that felt somewhat inappropriate, on the lips and too familiar. Beth continued smiling, paying no mind.

When Louise came to congratulate the newlyweds, the two sisters fell into each other's arms and cried.

"I can't help thinking about Papa," Louise whispered. "He would have been so proud of you."

"I know," Beth agreed, "Perhaps, he and Mama are looking down from heaven right now?"

"I'd like to think so," Louise murmured.

Thinking about the past brought memories and unanswered questions.

"You know, Louise, there's been something I've been meaning to ask you. Whatever happened to Dahlia and Fanny? I grew up with those two. They were my best friends. I saw them at church a few times, and then they were gone. I don't understand. Where are they? Did something bad happen?"

Louise's face went solemn. Feeling uneasy, she stared down at the ground as she spoke. "Honestly, I don't know. One day, they were both gone, on the same day that is. No one has any answers. There are plenty of rumors. The only one that makes any sense is that they were both sold. To whom or where, nobody seems to know. I'll keep my ear to the ground. If I hear of anything, I'll let you know."

This intimate moment stopped, as the revelry around them took control, and all were whisked away to the celebration.

****

They heard the music, as they approached the slave quarters. Coming closer, the aroma of the food made the crowd walk faster. Again, they placed flowers strategically all around. Opening the pit, the meat was perfectly prepared. Everywhere there were smiles.

Though dancing was forbidden on the plantation, it didn't stop folks from swaying to the music, moving up and down, back and forth to the rhythm. They even sang along whether they knew the words or not.

Even the elders in the crowd couldn't remember a celebration as grand as this. Everything went off as planned. Everything was memorable: the food, the music, the gathering.

Pastor Gaines stopped by to give the newlyweds his blessing, just in time for the cutting of the cake.

At sunset, they began to clean up and head back to their homes. Wedding or not, tomorrow was to be an early workday. Such things never change.

Again, all goodnights were accompanied by congratulations: handshakes, hugs, and kisses.

It was time for Louise to return to the Colby Plantation. The sisters held onto each other in tears.

"I'm so happy for you, Beth."

"I love you, Louise, and one day I will be your Matron of Honor, real soon, you'll see."

To Beth's relief, James volunteered to escort Louise home. To James' disappointment, Victor decided to accompany them.

Standing alone in the center of the slave quarters, Beth and Gray held hands, smiling at each other.

"Tell me who are you?" Beth asked with gentle love.

"I am your slave," Gray answered with full resolve.

"Where have you come from?" she asked.

"From the beginning of time to find you…"

"How long have you been searching?"

"Forever…"

"Now that you've found me, how long will you stay?"

"Till the end of time…"

Taking her by the hand, he guided her to their new home.

15

In All Honesty

Entering their new home, Beth nearly broke down in tears. The house was decorated with lit candles and flowers everywhere.

"Did you do this?" she asked Gray.

"…with the help of my brothers," he replied, smiling with pride.

She reached over and kissed him.

"That's not all," he said, taking her by the hand into the bedroom. Next to the bed, on a nightstand, candles burned softly. Shadows danced about the walls and on the ceiling. Someone sprawled a handful of red rose peddles over the bed.

Again, taking her by the hand, he guided her to the kitchen table. On it were fresh made sweets.

"Oh, no," Beth said, laughing. "I couldn't eat another bite."

Gray took up a clear bottle, holding it next to his smiling face. "How about we have a small taste?"

"Taste of what?"

He uncorked the bottle and poured small amounts into two glasses. "Moonshine, I don't know about you, but I could use a glass."

"I don't drink," she countered

"Me neither," he said, "but I'm a little nervous."

Beth was nervous, too, however not of the night. Thoughts of her father, how he drank after the death of her mother. How moonshine turned him into a wild beast of a man. Thankfully, eventually he quite, but it was too late to save his life.

As if he could read her mind, Gray placed the glass in her hand, and spoke softly to her. "You're not your father, Beth, you never will be. I've never met her, but I'd bet you're a lot like you mother."

They clinked glasses and sipped the liquor.

"It burns going down," remarked Beth.

"Yeah, but it's good, ain't it?"

She shrugged her shoulders, not knowing, and took another sip.

When they finished their drinks, Gray poured them another.

"Are you trying to get me drunk," she laughed.

"Just one more, it'll relax you."

Beth was never a drinker. She never understood it. It tastes bad and makes you act stupid. When she was halfway through the second glass, she began feeling strange. Not in a bad way, mind you, but different. When she got down to the bottom of the glass, everything changed, she changed, the world changed. Everything was the same only more so. She was happy, only now she seemed happier, in love, only more so.

Gray took her in his arms, and it felt so right. Slowly, he guided her back to the bedroom. They stood at the side of the bed, lost in each other. He backed away slightly, and undid the top button of her gown. She reached up and unbuttoned the top of his shirt. They both began laughing. It was their private celebration. Their fingers and hands were flying as buttons were unbuttoned and ties were untied. All the while kissing, and laughing between each kiss. In no time, they were naked, holding each other close. Without warning, Gray pushed her onto the bed, jumping on top of her. They hugged, kissed, rolling about laughing.

They kissed deeply, and the laughter disappeared, replaced by passion. Gray's hands explored her and hers him. The moonshine took over. The room rolled like a rowboat out at sea.

"I love you so much," whispered Gray.

There was so much Beth wanted to say, except all that came out was, "I love you, too."

Gray rose, looking down at her. "I have a confession to make," he said solemnly.

It seemed like an awkward time for an admission, except the look in his eyes told her how important it was to him. So, she listened intensely.

The moonshine took hold and began steering him into deep waters. "This is not the first time for me," he said. "I have to tell you, I'm not a virgin. I've done this before."

Again, Beth wasn't sure of the point of the conversation; still, Gray continued.

"There were three other women before you. I won't mention their names. It's not necessary. Besides, two of them still live here on the plantation. So, I don't think you need to know who they are.

"I do want you to know that it was only physical. I was young, and they meant nothing to me. Nothing like what's between you and me. There was no love there. I love you with all my heart. You must never be jealous. There will never be another woman in my life other than you. I swear."

When he'd seemingly gotten it all off his chest, he went silent.

For whatever reason, unknown to her, Beth felt moved to come clean, as well. It started as a spark deep within her and slowly became a roaring fire. Perhaps, the moonshine had something to do with it. Gray's sincerity moved her. She too wanted to start their life together on an honest note.

"I have a confession to make, too," she said softly, sounding afraid to speak above a whisper. Gray backed away just a little more, looking inquisitively at her.

"This isn't my first time, either," Beth blurted out. "It was at the last plantation I lived at."

Somewhere in the back of her mind, she decided not to name any names. Her logic was: the least he knew the better. Besides, he didn't name his lovers, why should she?

She continued, "It was just one man. He was my first and only one. There were no others."

Gray moved away, sitting on the edge of the bed, looking hurt.

Beth sat up, throwing her arms around him. "But it wasn't love…never, it was nothing like what we have."

"How long did it last?" he asked.

"Longer than I wanted it to. I never wanted it to start, in the first place."

"Why…were you raped?"

This was not a question Beth expected, nor did she have a good answer for.

"Not exactly," she replied, believing it was the best answer, and as close to the truth as she dare go.

"What do you mean, 'Not exactly'?"

Another question she needed time to think of a good answer.

"I didn't exactly try to fight him off."

"Why not…?"

"There was no point in trying to fight him off. He was determined to have his way. There was nothing I could do. So I resolved to just let it happen and try to live through it."

"How did it end?" he asked.

"I begged him to let me go. I suppose he took pity on me. Finally, he sold me to the Tanners."

In that moment, Beth realized how she foolishly told him the other man's name.

"So, it was Collin Townsend?" he said, as much a statement as a question.

"That's not all of it," Beth sobbed. "I had a child by him."

"Where's the child now?"

"I don't know. He never even told me if it was a boy or a girl. As soon as I had the child, he sold it to another plantation. I have no idea where."

Beth could feel she was losing Gray.

He gently broke free of her arms, took up his clothes and left the room. Beth wrapped a sheet around her, and followed him into the kitchen. There she found him putting on his clothes. His back was to her.

"Gray, what are you doing?"

It took him a moment to answer. He silently dressed. Not till he was seated putting on his shoes did he answer her.

"I can't do this, Beth. It would eat me up inside. It's already starting to."

"Gray, what are saying?"

"I can't be with you, knowing you've been with another man."

"I was just being honest with you. You told me of your past, and it doesn't matter to me."

"It's different with a man. I thought you were pure. The images in my mind won't stop. They won't give me peace."

"Why is it different for a man?" Beth shouted, clearly angry. "Why is it all right for you to have a past, and not me? I listened to your experiences and then immediately forgot them. Why did you tell them to me in the first place, if they're so unimportant?"

"I wanted to be honest," he whimpered, tying the laces of his shoes.

"Oh, my honesty doesn't count. My past is written in stone and burrows deep into your heart. Well, it's not your heart, Gray; it's your selfish pride."

He stood up, still unable to look into her face.

She realized going back and forth and criticizing him would get them nowhere. She changed her approach.

"Gray, look at me, for God's sake, please, look at me," she begged, tears rolling down her cheeks.

Slowly, he turned his head to look at her. It was as he thought. That lovely face covered in tears tore into his heart.

"Gray, I love you and I believe you know that. I believe you love me, too. Come back to bed. Let me help you forget both our pasts."

Now, his eyes were watering up. "I do love you. I can't deny that. Still, I can't erase these images in my mind. Forgive me. I have to go."

He started for the door. Beth leaped forward, the sheet fell off her. Naked, she fell to her knees, reaching out, wrapping her arms around his legs, hoping to stop him.

"Gray, please…"

"Forgive me, Beth. I have to go."

He gently pried her arms off him.

"Please, Beth, don't make this more difficult than it needs to be."

"I'm making this more difficult?" she questioned his logic. "You're ruining both our lives."

"I'm sorry. Perhaps, in time I'll change. But I can't," he said, opening the door. As he closed the door, he made a last request. "Pray for me."

She leaned on the door. She heard the wood of the porch creak as he left, and him running in the dust outside. He was gone.

Beth remained sprawled on the floor naked and crying for the longest time. Then she rose to her feet, unaware or not caring of her nakedness, she left the sheet on the floor. Walking to the table, she lifted the half-full bottle of moonshine. She carried it back with her to the bedroom.

16

Consummate

When Beth woke, she wasn't in bed. She lay on the floor, naked, and an empty bottle of moonshine in her hand. Her head was pounding, everything hurt. She swore even the ends of her hair were injured.

She was in no shape to go to work, and she'd be late if she did. Then she remembered that Mr. and Mrs. Tanner gave her and Gray the day off from work to celebrate their wedding. That thought lead to a string of memories.

The recollection of the night before flooded her mind, every vision, every word echoed within her. The conversation between Gray and her continued over and over; and each time it felt more and more hopeless.

She rose from the floor, found her clothes and dressed. Sitting at the table, drinking coffee, she couldn't stop thinking.

Gossip sweeps over a plantation fast and hard like an ocean wave crashes against the rocks. Surely by now, most of the others knew what happened between her and Gray; if not in detail, at least that something was wrong. By sunset, everyone would know. How could she ever face the world again? Could she ever hold up her head? For this reason, she remained within, sulking. Before she knew it, the day was over; the shack fell into darkness. A wave of shame came over her.

Here she was wasting the day away feeling sorry for herself. What about Gray? What must he be going through? She never meant to hurt him; still, he was hurt, and she was the cause. She would make things right again. How…she didn't know. But, she needed to try.

She laid out her clothes for the morning, washed up, combed out her hair, and returned to bed. To sleep, only this time, to wake rested, get through the day, and find a way to get Gray back.

****

Beth woke bright and early with new hope in her heart. Walking to the main house, she was well aware of the stares of others. She paid them no mind.

She spent the entire day lost in her work, ignoring and being ignored by the other house workers. It may seem foolish, she couldn't shake off the feeling that any moment Gray would show up, or send word to her. But it never happened.

At the end of the day, Beth walked home through the slave quarters. Passing by her old home where now Victor and James lived, she could only believe Gray was there, too. After all, where else would he go?

The temptation was too great, and she wasn't about to let her smugness get in the way. She swallowed her pride, walked onto the porch, and knocked on the door.

The door opened slowly, inwardly she hoped it was Gray, only, it was James who stood in the doorway.

"James…is Gray here?" she asked.

"No he's not, Beth. We haven't seen him. We heard that something's wrong between you two. But he hasn't been here. We don't know where he is."

"If you do see him, tell him I need to speak with him."

"Yes, of course." She was just about to walk away when James reached out to her, taking her hand. "Beth, I'm sorry. I don't know what happened between you two. Do you wanna talk about it?"

"Thanks, but, I need to talk with Gray."

"I understand," he said, letting go of her hand. "He's probably out somewhere thinking things over. Don't worry, he'll be back. If I see him, I'll tell him you called."

Beth nodded with a half smile, turned and walked away.

****

Days turned into weeks, and still no sight of or word from Gray. Beth took life one day and one step at a time. It was interesting to see how people treated her; they ignored her. The rule of thumb being: don't get involved, and you will avoid trouble. Whether what happened was Beth's fault, Gray's fault, or the fault of both of them, it didn't matter. It was trouble and to be shunned at all cost. Life is hard enough without inviting it in.

At the end of each day, Beth walked through the slave quarters to her home. And as she passed her old home, knowing Gray was most possibly in there, she felt tempted to knock on the door. It took all her strength to walk on.

It was on one particular evening, from a distance she saw a man waiting on her porch. Her first thought and hope was that it was Gray. Coming closer, disappointment crashed down on her like an avalanche. It wasn't Gray; it was his older brother, Victor.

"Beth," he greeted her, tipping his hat at the brim.

"Victor…wasn't excepting you."

"Could we step inside, Beth?" he asked, pointing to her front door. "I've got something to talk to you about."

Hoping it had something to do with Gray; she rushed up the stairs to let both of them in.

"Please, sit down," said Beth, pointing to a chair at the table. "Would you like something to drink?"

He shook his head.

Beth took a seat across from Victor, silently waiting for what he had to say.

"First let me say, we know you and Gray had a falling-out. There's much guesswork going on with everyone, except, no one knows for sure. Gray refuses to talk about it."

"Then he's living with you?" Beth asked.

"Yes, sooner or later he had to come home. That's the reason I'm here today. As the oldest, I guess you can say I'm the elder of the family, so I need to say this. I hope whatever's goin' on between you and Gray, whatever you two are dealing with, I hope that someday you can resolve it and get back together. Except, meanwhile, three men living in such a small space will never do. We moved you into our larger home because we figured it the right thing to do with you and Gray getting together and maybe startin' a family, and all. It just ain't workin'. We need to switch back."

Beth didn't so much as try to hide the disappointment she felt. This was not the conversation she was hoping to have. Instead of getting back together, she and Gray were moving farther apart.

"When do you plan to do this?" she asked.

"Tomorrow after work, my brothers and I will deliver our things here, and then we will take your things to your old home. However, there is one condition."

"What's that?"

"Gray asked that you not be around. He doesn't want to see you."

Inwardly, Beth thought this to be a petty and childish request. Nevertheless, she kept it to herself, knowing it would get back to Gray; and hurtful words were not needed now, and counter to her intentions.

Victor continued, "When you see all your things outside your old home, James and I will bring them in the house and arrange them any way you like."

Beth sighed, "I guess I could continue to work passed my usual time. I doubt anyone will complain, least of all the Tanners."

"Then it's settled…tomorrow," Victor said, rising from his chair and making for the door. "I'm sorry it turned out this way for you, Beth," he murmured as he left, closing the door behind him.

17

Something Awful

"Why, Beth, why are you still here?" Mrs. Tanner asked.

"These glasses could use a wiping."

"Oh, that can wait until tomorrow. You've got a husband you need to go home to and cook for."

No words were said or needed; one look at Beth's face and the old woman knew something was wrong.

"Beth, what is the matter?"

It took a moment for Beth to answer and do it without crying. "We're no longer together."

"My word, when did this happen?"

"On our wedding night, words were said between us, and he left me."

Mrs. Tanner burst into laughter. "My dear, if I had a penny for every time Mr. Tanner and I had words with each other, I'd be a rich woman. You go straight home, you cook him a fine dinner and have a nice sit down talk. It'll all be better in the morning."

"It's not like that, ma'am. It's serious."

"Of course, it is," she laughed. "It's always serious. Now you go home and do as I say. You know what the problem is? You blacks don't have enough God in your lives."

"We were married in a church!" Beth spouted, sounding a bit cantankerous.

"Maybe so, except I know you folks carry around some of those old country superstitions into your beliefs. What you people need is the Lord in your lives."

Beth let out a long sigh. She could think of a million arguments to this way of thinking. Only, she knew the old woman meant well and would not listen. They say, '*You can't teach an old dog new tricks*'. What Beth was confronted with was an old dog.

Wearing a motherly smile, Mrs. Tanner took the glass from Beth, placed her hands on the young woman's shoulders and spun her around to face the door. "Now, you get on home, and you take my advice. It'll all be better in the morning. And remember, *the way to a man's heart is through his stomach*."

As Beth stepped out of the main house, she shook her head, amazed at how little the old woman understood, or did she? The part about having a sit down, bring it all out into the open, and talking it out, might well be sound advice.

****

Approaching her old home, which now was to be her home once more, she saw all her things placed on the porch. The three brothers stood side by side, talking. Beth jumped behind a bush, to observe. She felt persuaded to come right out in the open and approach Gray, only, she decided it the wrong thing to do at the time.

Victor and James remained on the porch, as Gray left. Beth watched him walk away. It was easy to see how hard the separation hurt and damaged him. His eyes were red and sunken from nights of little to no sleep. His hair was wild and unkempt. His clothes looked as if he hadn't changed them in days.

When he'd gone, Beth stepped out from behind the bush, walking to the brothers. James nodded to her, Victor moved forward.

"We've got all your things here. Just tell us where you want them."

Inside, Beth pointed out where to put everything. There wasn't much to move; the two men had it done in no time. She walked them out, and they stood on the porch.

"You take care of yourself, you hear?" James said, reaching out and shaking hands with Beth. They both instantly realized what a pointless and embarrassing gesture this was. Still, awkward moments make for foolish actions.

"Thank you," Beth told them.

"If there's anything you need, you just say so," said Victor. "Despite the way things seem right now, you're still family."

Beth smiled, moved by his words.

"There is one thing you can do for me."

"What's that?" Victor asked.

"Tell Gray…" She stopped for a moment. There was so much she wanted to say. "Tell him I love him."

****

The loneliness and the sadness weighted heavy on Beth. Days flowed into one another, impossible to tell apart.

There were a few times when she watched the fields from afar and thought she saw Gray working off in the distance, yet she wasn't sure. There was no sign of him. Each night she waited in the dark, dreaming of a tap at the door and if it would be him. Weeks went by with never a knock.

Sundays at church, there wasn't a sign of him or his brothers. Nor was there ever a sign of her two friends Fanny and Dahlia. No one could give her a word about what happened to them or their whereabouts. It was as if they'd disappeared from the earth.

Most often, her sister, Louise, came and they'd sit together. When she heard of the separation, on the wedding night no less, Louise was heartbroken.

"I don't understand it," said Louise. "You both seemed so happy and in love. And to break up on your wedding night…"

"These things happen," was the short answer from Beth. Honestly, she didn't want to discuss it. Realizing this, Louise dropped the subject.

For no particular reason, Beth took a good long look at her sister, something she hadn't done in a while. The child in Louise was missing. Her cuteness had turned to beauty. She was, for all purposes, a lovely woman.

"Do you have a boy in your life?" Beth asked.

"What?" Louise said in surprise. "I'm too young for boys."

"I doubt the boys would agree with you," Beth laughed.

Louise looked down with embarrassment.

****

It was the middle of the night, late. There was a knock at the door. Beth ignored it. She'd dreamed of Gray knocking at her door so many times, she could not bear waking to another disappointment. So, she turned over.

When there was another knock, she realized it was not a dream. There really was someone at the door. Wrapping her robe tightly around her, she went to answer.

It would be a lie to say she didn't have butterflies in her stomach, hoping it was Gray on the other side of the door. If it was true, she wouldn't say a word, only burst out crying and fall into his arms. Still, there was another part of her, warning her not to get her hopes up too high, preparing her for disappointment.

With a trembling hand she opened the door. It was Victor, standing in the doorway with his hat in his hand.

"Victor, it's the middle of the night. Is something wrong? Is Gray all right?"

"Oh, he's fine. He don't even know I'm here, nobody does. Can I come in? We need to talk."

"I'm going to make some coffee; would you like some?" Beth asked.

"Yes, that would be nice," he replied, sitting down at the table.

Placing the coffees down, Beth took a seat across from Victor.

"Thank you," Victor said softly, and then taking a sip.

"So, Victor, tell me, what's so important that it couldn't wait until morning?"

He stared deep into the black of the coffee, silent for a moment, and then speaking in a gentle tone. "It's about you and Gray."

"What about me and Gray?"

"I spoke with him and he refused to talk about it, not a word. I have no idea what went wrong between you two. But I want you to know I've tried many times to talk him into coming back to you. I'm afraid it's never going to happen."

His words shot through her heart like an arrow.

"Victor, I appreciate you telling me this, I really do. Only, like I asked before, why couldn't this wait for the morning?"

"Well, there's more to it than that," he mumbled shyly.

Beth remained silent, waiting for the rest the story.

"Like I said, I tried to get Gray to see the error of his ways, but he won't have any of it. Then I think of you alone, trying to make a life for yourself. My heart goes out to you. You're a good woman, Beth, and you shouldn't be treated like this. You need a good man to love you and look after you. And I think…"

He stopped for a moment, the words caught in his throat.

"And I think I could be that man."

A shocked look shot across Beth's face. She wasn't sure what to do. She felt like running away. It was clear she wasn't pleased, as she shook her head.

"Think about it, Beth. Gray's not mature enough for a woman. He's still a boy, in many ways. I could take care of you. I could make you happy."

Beth fell into deep thought. She understood rejection, how deeply it hurts. Victor was not the man for her; still, she didn't want to hurt him. She would choose her words slowly and carefully.

"Victor, I'm a married woman."

"No one believes that! Where is your husband? You've been abandoned. No one recognizes your marriage, not even the reverend that performed the ceremony. You need to move on, Beth; and there's no reason you need to remain alone. We could be so happy, Beth."

As much as she wanted to be kind, she decided to nip it in the bud.

"Victor, you're a very kind man, and I do so respect you, except I don't think of you in that way. I'm married to Gray, and I'll wait for him for as long as it takes."

"But he's not coming back," Victor insisted.

"I don't believe that's true," she replied. "I have to believe he will."

Victor remained seated, staring forward, looking right through her.

"Victor, I'm sorry, but it's the middle of the night."

This didn't seem to affect him in the least. It was as if he hadn't heard. Beth's voice remained gentle, only now more resolved.

"Victor, it's late; you have to leave."

He rose from his chair. Believing he was about to leave, Beth stood up to walk him to the door. When he didn't move and continued to stare, Beth became uncomfortable.

"Victor, are you all right?"

Without warning, Victor leaped at Beth like a wild beast, grabbing her by the shoulders. The next moment, he was kissing her. The initial shock caused her to stiffen and freeze up. Then she began to fight back, wriggling, trying to escape his grasp, only, he was far too strong for her to break free.

He removed his lips from hers, moving his mouth along the length of her neck. Pulling the material of her nightgown off her shoulders, he began kissing them, then back up her neck, and again locking onto her mouth.

She squirmed and tried desperately to break free, to no avail. Her moans were the guttural sounds of fear, anger, and disgust, which only seemed to fan the flames of his passion.

She began crying, her tears wetting his face, as well. It had no affect on him, his infatuation was all consuming.

Ever so slowly, he guided her backwards till she felt the back of her legs pressing against her bed.

His hands were all over her, exploring. Gradually, he grabbed fistfuls of her clothing, tearing them away. The sound of the ripping was like the shrieks of small children. On and on he tore till she stood before him naked.

His strong arms grabbed her, tossing her down onto the bed. She lay there in tears, looking at him, unable to make eye contact. He undid the front of his pants, and then fell upon her like a cold snowdrift.

She'd been here before, this was nothing new. She lived through many a dark night with Collin. In those days, she learned to survive by simply shutting down her mind. It was time to do the same.

There was a safe space somewhere in the back of her mind. She was just about to crawl into it and lock it shut, when suddenly a hand grabbed Victor by the hair, pulling him off her.

They dragged him not just off her but off the bed and across the room. Victor went flying, falling to the floor, hitting his head against the stove.

In the dim light, Beth couldn't tell who Victor's attacker was, only that she saw the outline of a man. There was a stirring in her like an inward storm. She hoped and prayed her savior was Gray.

Victor growled as he rose to his feet, the front of his trousers still open wide. There was a large kitchen knife next to the stove. He took it, slowly approaching his assailant. The other man took hold of one of the chairs, holding it over his head.

"Put the knife down, Victor," said the man.

Victor stopped in his tracks, growling.

"Put it down, Victor; don't make me hit you. You're older and bigger than me, anyways, you know I can put up one hell of a fight. Either way, win or lose, this isn't going to end well. Put it down, Victor."

Victor backed up slightly, returning the knife to where he found it.

Although the voice was familiar, it wasn't until the moonlight oozing through the window struck his face and she realized it was James.

"I don't want to fight you, Victor. Just go home and we'll forget about all of this."

Victor didn't move, catching his breath. Eventually, he seemed calm enough to reason with.

"This isn't like you, Victor. Button the front of you trousers."

A look of shame came over Victor, as he buttoned up.

"I'm sorry," Victor moaned like a child afraid of the dark, seeking the assuring voice of an adult. "Please, forgive me." He started for the door.

James finally put down the chair. He called out to Victor, just before he left.

"Oh, and, Victor, you're my brother and I love you, but if you ever come to Beth and try something like this again, I'll kill you."

With that Victor left. It wasn't till they could no longer hear his footsteps that James turned toward Beth. The first thing he did was take hold of the bedcovers and bring them up over her.

"I'm sorry about that," he said. "You'll have to forgive Victor. I've never seen him like that. Then again, living your life, even with two brothers, is like living alone, and loneliness can treat you something awful."

Beth slowly calmed till finally she could speak.

"Thank you, James," was all she could get out.

"Are you all right?" he asked.

"I'll be fine. Thank you, again."

An awkward moment of silence passed between them. Deciding it was best to leave, he turned and headed for the door. Standing in the doorway, he made a proclamation that gave wings to her heart.

"Gray loves you very much. I know this. He's told me many times how much he loves you. I've no idea what's the matter with him. Sometimes he makes me so angry. Don't give up, Beth. I'm gonna talk with him. I'll knock some sense into that thick skull of his, if I have to. He'll be back one day, I just know it."

He was just about to leave when an idea echoed back in his mind.

"Like I said, you gotta forgive Victor. Loneliness can do some strange things to a body."

"I know," Beth said, being of the same mind.

James left, closing the door.

18

Lost Souls

Weeks later, there still was no sign of Gray. Thankfully, there also was no sign of Victor, and sadly none of James. However, there were a few mornings when Beth walked to the main house and in the evenings going home, Beth saw Gray off in the distance, working in the fields. Even from a distance, she recognized him, she knew his outline like the back of her hand. Many were the times she wanted to walk out into the fields and confront him. If she was certain it would do any good, she would.

It was in early autumn when it still looked of summer, only the heat wasn't as severe, and a person with a concerning eye could see the subtle changes that lead to winter. Mrs. Tanner gathered all the household workers in the parlor.

"Starting today, all of you will not only be working for me, you will be working for God. There is a war being fought between good and evil. The Lord is the general leading us, and we are all soldiers in his army, and we must follow without question.

"The Lord has laid it on my heart to do what little I can in this battle against Satan. In three weeks, my husband and I will host a revival here on the Tanner property. It will last for two days. Well-known Christian orators and lecturers, both locale and international, will be speaking on the Good Word. Many will attend from far and wide.

"Now, I know all of you work hard each day, only, I'm asking you to go that extra mile. As well as souls to be saved, there will be mouths to be fed. That's were you come in. Not just for me, do it for the Lord."

The house staff stood smiling, the smile they knew would appease the powers that be, namely Mrs. Tanner. It was an acquired smile, taking many years to learn, and passed down from generation to generation.

****

They'd separated the Tanner Plantation into seven fields. Each year, one of the fields went unattended, no plowing, planting, or sowing, a year of rest. This tradition can be found in the Old Testament, although, no one but the Tanners heard of it, including the local pastors.

It was the year of rest for the front east field. They brought in hired workers to flatten the field. Above and beyond their normal daily duties, the house staff prepared and served food for these extra men.

Flattening the field was only the beginning. On the site, they erected small tents. It takes numerous people to put on a revival. These tents would house them. When all the tents were up, it looked like an army camp.

As for the orators scheduled to speak, they'd have top accommodations: a room in the main house, their meals taken with the Tanners.

Next was the main tent, larger than three churches, able to seat hundreds. It took a full two days to erect. Chairs were delivered and set up, as was a large stage at one end of the tent.

In the three weeks leading up to the revival, the Tanners were deeply involved with spreading the news. They sent invitations to churches throughout the state and beyond. They journeyed within the county to churches, making public appearances to drum up more interest. All looked well, it seemed attendance would be better than anyone could hope or pray for.

In a dream, Mrs. Tanner saw a vision of hundreds of people entering the tent, walking under a banner that read: *Crusade for Lost Souls*. From that moment on, that was the name given to the revival. The next morning, a large banner stating so was ordered in bloodred satin with gold lettering and fringe.

****

Those scheduled to speak were as follows: Reverend Peterson, pastor of the local Methodist church. He was to be the narrator for both days, keeping the crowd interested between speakers, and doing the introductions.

J.R.T. Redding an evangelist, an up-and-coming speaker throughout the tristate area would be the opener on the first day, followed by Keith Stubbs, known for his strong emotional, tear soaked sermons.

The first day would end with a full two hour sermon from Emmanuel Forrester, the internationally known and respected evangelist, truly the star of the crusade.

The plan for the second day started with two local preachers: Bishop Rieslings formally of Massachusetts, known for his Biblical knowledge, able to quote scripture at the drop of a hat. After seminary, he and his wife moved to the South, and lived there since.

The second speaker, another local, went by the name of The Apostle Bill. He'd lived the first part of his life as a savage pagan. After finding religion, he turned his life around. This was the bulk of his sermons.

Finally, the day would conclude with another two hours of Emmanuel Forrester.

The time between speakers was to be well-spent with music. Not just any music, heavenly music, hymns and songs of praise intended to move the heart and lift the spirit. The *Miller Orchestra and Choir* came all the way from Atlanta. They consisted of mostly drums, woodwinds, and brass, no strings. The Miller Choir was a thirty member choir of both male and female singers, bass, baritone, soprano, and alto. All of this conducted by Mitchell Miller Esquire, performing the most inspiring and holy music this side of the pearly gates.

As if that was not enough, Sister Sara would be on hand, singing with the Miller Orchestra and Choir. Though up in years, her voice was as strong as ever. Her reputation as the *Angel of Praise* proceeded her throughout the South.

With the amount of reservations received, The *Hampton House* and the *Enchanted Huntsman*, the two hotels in town, would be full not only during the crusade, but two days before and after.

As for other accommodations, many of the other farms and plantations walking distance to the Tanner property put up signs that folks could camp on their property for a nominal charge.

The fee for the crusade was quite reasonable, although the cost of many of the other amenities could add up to a pretty penny. The cash split was as such: The entry fees as well as the sales of food and drink would all go to the Tanners, in hopes of reimbursing their many expenses and sacrifices. The sales of Bibles, souvenirs, and donations, which they hoped to be much, all of it went to the Emmanuel Forrester Mission, which paid the musicians, singers, and speakers' wages agreed on in advance.

****

Two days before the crusade, the air was electric. People flooded into the region. The musicians and singers arrived; they began rehearsing immediately. Supplies arrived. The house staff began preparing the food for the workers and what they'd serve the multitude – for a price, of course. There were also barrels of sweet cider to be tapped into – for sale.

Late in the afternoon, most of the preachers and Emmanuel Forrester arrived and shown to their rooms, excluding the local speakers.

As for Emmanuel Forrester, in the evening when he appeared, it was like the parting of the red sea mixed with the second coming. Everyone was in awe of the man, close to swooning.

At first glance, Emmanuel Forrester was an unimpressive, ordinary middle-aged man in his fifties, slender, slightly graying at the temples. However, when he walked into the room, there was a charisma about him capturing everyone's attention. There was a calmness about him that seemed unreal, yet could not be faked. His voice was smooth and cutting, capturing the ears of all present. That evening, sitting at the dinner table, everyone remained silent, giving their full attention, hanging on his every word.

The next day they spent doing a dry run of what was to happen. Every detail was worked out.

By evening, the hotels were full, the camping grounds were full. Everything was in place.

That night's supper was a repeat of the night before. Everyone sat listening intensely to every word uttered by Emmanuel Forrester.

Meanwhile, Beth and the other staff ate and relaxed in the kitchen, discussing what happened and what they suspected would. All of them already felt exhausted, and the crusade hadn't even started.

****

The morning started early, before sunrise. Everyone got into place. Beth was to spend the day pouring glasses of sweet cider. Next to her were other slaves assigned to serve food. Some elderly women from the white church volunteered to collect the moneys for food and drink. A crew of young men was assigned to collecting the dirty dishes and glasses, bringing them to the kitchen, cleaning them, then bringing them back. As well, they replenished the food and drink. Going in, they knew this would be a nonstop hustle of a day.

At sunup, they let the people in. Every seat was taken in no time. The crowd doubled by folks standing on the edge of the tent's perimeter.

Reverend Peterson greeted the crowd, saying a few words getting the crowd to settle down, grabbing everyone's interest. Then the music began. This put everyone in the mood.

J.R.T. Redding was the first to speak, a calming little man with a voice that could sooth a tiger. He didn't so much as preach as told the crowd what to expect for the next two days, especially from Emmanuel Forrester. If he said it once, he must have mentioned the man's name a hundred times. It was clear he was priming the crowd, giving them hope and expectation.

Once Redding finished, the music began, again. Folks who didn't have enough time to breakfast at their hotel, and those who woke too late to eat something at their campsites, made their way to the food counters. Of course, some sweet cider would be the perfect drink to wash it all down. Beth was pouring nonstop. If this was any indication what was about to happen, a small sample of what lunch would be like, it was going to be a long difficult day.

Keith Stubbs had his own style of preaching, different from Redding. He had them moved to tears in no time. *Hallelujahs* and *Amen* filled the air. Arms waved about, tears fell; the spirit was moving.

When Stubbs concluded, it was passed one o'clock. The crowd felt elevated, exhausted, and hungry. The lines for food and drink were long. When Beth placed down a glass of cider, it was snatched up as soon as touching the table. This feeding frenzy went on for nearly an hour.

When it was over and everyone sat quiet and content, the music started again, only this time it was lead by Sister Sara. At first, it was easy to say she had a pleasant and well-trained voice. Yet, as the song progressed she began hitting notes only meant for trumpets and angels. The spirit moved closer.

On her last song, the last note was high and long. As it filled the tent, Emmanuel Forrester appeared onstage, seemingly out of nowhere. The crowd jumped to their feet, some stood on their chairs, clapping and cheering, drowning out the sound of the music. This ovation lasted for nearly three minutes.

Forrester's approach to preaching was explosive. Within the first minute, he had them in the palm of his hand. His voice was powerful, always speaking in a singsong manner, repeating key phrases over and over till you could hear them echoing in your mind with no escaping it. He pranced across the stage, back and forth, like a rooster in a henhouse.

The band began playing softly when he announced anyone with ailments could approach the stage. There would be laying of hands and prayers for healing. It was a parade of the hopeful, old and young, those needing help, some with canes, some with crutches, and some needing to be carried.

Behind these poor people was a sea of people wanting forgiveness and to be healed spiritually. Nearly everyone was in the line to the stage. Forrester laid hands on each, one by one. There were tears of joy, shouting and howling. Canes and crutches were thrown aside. Hands shook in the air. Folks fell to the ground, quivering as if having a seizure. It took quite a while; still, no one was turned away or disappointed.

Once everyone was seen to, Forrester was able to get everyone to return to their seats, a small miracle in itself.

"I'm sure all of you understand that crusades such as this don't happen out of thin air," Forrester proclaimed. "It takes dedication by many people, it takes hard work and sweat, and although no one likes to hear it, it takes money, lots of money."

An uncomfortable laughter rumbled through the crowd.

"You knew it was coming. The moment we ask for donations. And I have no doubt in my mind that you expected it and have put some money aside to give, and will give gladly and freely. Only, I have one question to ask all of you."

Silence prevailed.

"I have to ask where your faith is and where is your joy? Because, if you can't give with a joyous heart, and don't do it as an act of faith, we don't want your money. You may ask…'How do I do this?'…well, you look deep into your heart and find the joy that God put there. Think of all the things in life that make you happy, and open your heart when you give.

"As for it being an act of faith, there is only one way. I want you to reach into your purse, push aside that money you planned to give when you came here today. And I want you to take hold of the largest bill you have on you, that will be the amount you give. God gave you his best! Isn't it about time you give yours?"

With that, the band burst into music, the choir broke into songs of hosanna, lead by Sister Sara. The spirit abound.

They passed baskets through the crowd. At the halfway point, they had to stop and get new empty baskets, the others were full. All gave with joy the highest denomination of bill they had. Interesting, in most cases, many gave that as well as the amount they originally planned to give.

****

The next day started out as a mirror image of the previous day. The first two speakers would be different; however, the day would end with Emmanuel Forrester.

Bishop Rieslings, the first speaker, stayed true to his reputation as a Biblical scholar and historian. He quoted scripture, rattled off dates and names. All in all, the crowd respected him, however, they remained unmoved. These folks came with their hearts in their hands. Riesling was without emotion, a cold fish.

There was the usual angelic music, as everyone prepared for the appearance of The Apostle Bill. He was a mystery. All that was known about him was that he was new to the preaching circuit, in fact, new to religion. His speeches were all about his early life as a pagan, how he found religion and turned his life around. He was a local, living somewhere in the county, which was why he didn't stay at the Tanner's home.

Beth was busy pouring cider when The Apostle Bill hit the stage. She hardly had time to breathe, let alone look to see what the man looked like. Still, his voice caught her attention. It sounded so familiar.

Finally, she stopped for a moment and looked to the stage. Her knees went weak, and her head spun like a top. She braced against the table as she felt faint.

The Apostle Bill was none other than Collin Townsend, her once master, her once lover, the father of her child, and the source of all her misery.

19

All through the Night

The crusade may have been over; however, the extra detail work was not. A massive cleanup to get everything back to its original state was needed. This took three days.

That night, Beth lay on her bed exhausted, thankful not only that it was over, but that Mrs. Tanner gave everyone involved the next day off. She planned to sleep it away. Beth was too tired to even get up and remove her clothes. She closed her eyes, and gently drifted to sleep.

Except it was an uneasy sleep, filled with disturbing visions. She hadn't seen or thought about Collin for nearly two years. That meant her child, he or she, was two years old. Collin's face was before her, his laughter rang in her ears, till finally she woke. However, it wasn't the dreams that woke her; it was the knocking at her door.

As always, her first thought was perhaps it was Gray. She jumped from the bed, and rushed to the door. Opening the door, she could see the outline of a man haloed by moonlight. It wasn't Gray, nor was it James or Victor, it was Collin Townsend.

"What are you doing here? What do you want?" Beth spat out her words in anger, as she backed away.

"Please, Beth, give me a chance to explain," Collin pleaded.

"We've nothing to talk about, Collin."

"Not even about your son?" he asked.

Beth turned to stone, a frozen silence.

"I thought that might get your attention. Let me come in, Beth," he asked, walking forward. Once inside, she shut the door.

"I'm listening," she said coldly.

"First, let me say that I'm sorry I treated you badly. I should never have done that. I was wrong. You need to understand what I've been through."

"What you've been through…?" she snickered.

"Please, Beth, let me explain. All my life I lived for me only, a life of sin. Then a miracle happened. I found the Lord, or should I say He found me. All my evil ways are behind me, now. I'm trying to make things right. When I saw you from the stage, many things ran through my head. I felt bad about what I've done to you, and needed to ask your forgiveness. Also, when I saw you it brought up old feelings. I miss you so much, Beth. I've never been happy with any other woman except you. What can I do to get back in your good graces? What can I do to win you back?"

Beth shook her head, sighing and then chuckling slightly. "Collin, you still don't understand. You were never in my good graces. You can't win me back because I was never yours. You took from me without any thought about me. With you I was even less than a slave. You took my child away from me and sold it. It wasn't until tonight that I even knew if it was a boy or a girl. Now you tell me it's a boy, you've changed your ways, and you want me in your life."

"Beth, I don't blame you for being mad with me. I understand. I realize now how much I love you. Give me a chance to make things right again."

"And how do you intend to do that?"

"I can start by getting your son back to you."

All the while they spoke, Beth felt unsure of what Collin said. Her inner self wanted to turn him out. However, the prospect of regaining her son calmed her. She suffered much in the past, and would endure more if need be for this to become true.

"Don't say yes or no, Beth. Don't say a word. Let me show you how I will treat you. Let me prove my love for you. Give me a week. I promise by that time, you will be reunited with your son. Then you will know."

He reached out for her, wanting so much to touch her; however, he knew he needed to prove himself to her first. He opened the door and left.

She could hear him whisper over his shoulder, as he faded into the night, "You'll see!"

She didn't know what to think, as she closed the door. All she knew was she hadn't felt this hopeful in a long time.

****

Three days later, after a day of work, Beth came home to find a wagon outside her house. Two large men were placing a crib on her front porch.

"What's going on?" Beth asked.

They turned in shock, like thieves, only they weren't taking away, they were bringing.

"Is your name Beth?" asked one of the men.

"Yes, how can I help you?"

"We got orders to deliver this crib. We were goin' to leave it on your porch, but since you're here, we'll put it wherever you want it."

Beth was lost in surprise. Was Collin going to follow through with his promise?

Stepping onto the porch, opening the door, she pointed to her bed. "You can leave it next to the bed, please."

The two men did just as she asked. Bowing out, they smiled. "If Master Collin asks, tell him we did just fine."

"Of course, I will. Thank you, both."

****

A week after Collin's visit, to the day and the hour, there was a knock on Beth's door. Collin stood in the doorway with a child, a two year old boy, on his hip.

"Beth, this is your son."

She stood staring, speechless. She remained unwavering till he handed the child to her. Due to the lateness of the hour, the child was asleep.

"His name is Ambrose," Collin said, entering. "I see you received the crib. It would be best to put him down. If we wake him, he's sure to fuss."

Beth placed him in his crib. They both stood over him, admiring this perfect child. He was light skinned, clearly a creation of mixed races. There was much of Collin in the boy. That was easy to see. Still, the shape of his eyes and his long lashes were unmistakably hers.

"Where has he been?" Beth asked in a whisper.

"I sold him to a plantation far away. He was raised by more than one wet nurse. It's about time he knew a mother's love."

Looking up, Beth had to ask, "Why are you doing this?"

"Like I said, I was a pagan, selfish. When I found religion, I not only went about preaching, I've tried to make all the wrongs I've done right again, just like Zacchaeus in the Bible. Then when I saw you from the stage, my heart went out to you in two ways. I not only wanted to make your life better, I wanted you back in my life. You never know what you have till you lose it."

"So, now you've given me back my child, and you expect me to return to you."

"No, Beth, no, I wish it were that easy. I didn't do this for you to pay me back with your love. I did this so you'll see that I've changed, and in time maybe you can love the new me."

He had nothing to add to this, and she had nothing to say. After placing a small bag of coins on the table, he turned and walked to the door.

"Bless this house, and this child and mother," he prayed as he left. "I'll be in touch," he said as he walked out into the night.

Alone, Beth looked down on Ambrose with disbelief. This was her child, her son. She bent low, kissing him on the forehead. Taking in a deep breath, there was a sweet fragrance about him. There was a beauty and strength in his face. Or perhaps, this is what all children look like through the eyes of a mother. Holding up the candle, she inspected his face carefully.

"You surely are your father's child."

****

Early next morning, Ambrose woke to a new world. He looked around confused. Still, nothing upset him; he appeared to take it all in stride. They stared at each other for the longest time. An easygoing child, he accepted her with little question. In no time they were both smiling and laughing. She scrambled an egg and feed him.

Ambrose cooed and giggled, though not anything that sounded like a word came from him, not one syllable. She thought this strange. Perhaps, his inability to speak was caused by the trauma of a motherless life. But she would soon change that.

She took him to the shack of one of the elderly women that took care of children while their parents worked the day in the fields. The woman told her, she already had two children she was looking after and didn't want a third. This is where the money Collin gave her came in handy. A few coins placed in the middle of the old woman's palm changed her mind.

Like lightening striking a field of dry grass, word of Beth having a son scorched across the plantation. By the end of the day, few folks hadn't heard the news.

Beth walked briskly towards the slave quarters. She couldn't wait to see Ambrose, again. It was then she noticed something different about herself, something had changed. She was happy. She hadn't felt glad to be alive for such a long time. There was a spring in her step, a smile on her face, and a fire in her belly. There was now a reason for living, and it felt wonderful.

When she entered the old woman's home, Ambrose was seated on the floor, playing with a pair of spoons.

"Ambrose," she called out. The boy looked up, and like a gift from God, he smiled up at her. It had only been one day, and already he recognized her.

All eyes followed her, as she marched to her home with Ambrose on her hip. It didn't matter. She ignored every one of them. She had her life back, and she was going to live it.

"What do you feed a baby?" she asked in her mind. "I've got to ask someone tomorrow. I guess oatmeal is fine."

That's what she did. On the stove, she slow cooked oatmeal till it was soft as melted butter. Feeding him was an experience, having to wipe from his lips what never made it into his mouth. He seemed more interested in things other than eating.

Later, she sat in her rocking chair, Ambrose in her arms. She sang softly to him.

Sleep my child and peace attend thee
All through the night
Guardian angels God will send thee
All through the night
Soft the drowsy hours are creeping
Hill and dale in slumber sleeping
I my loved one's watch am keeping
All through the night

Angels watching ever round thee
All through the night
In thy slumbers close surround thee
All through the night
They will of all fears disarm thee
No forebodings should alarm thee
They will let no peril harm thee
All through the night
*

When she finished, she placed the sleeping child, her son, Ambrose, in his crib.

*Edward Jones 1784

20

No Tomorrow

Beth couldn't remember when she enjoyed living as much as she did over the next few weeks. As monotonous and routine as it was, it didn't matter. At the end of the day, it was Ambrose and her, and that's all that mattered.

On one particular day walking home, Beth sensed someone creeping up on her. The faster she walked, the faster were the steps behind her. Finally, she decided the best thing to do was stop and confront whomever it was. She spun around only to be confronted with a familiar face.

"James, you scared me half to death, why didn't you say something?"

"Sorry, I wasn't thinking. Do you have a minute? I've got something to talk to you about."

She waited for him to go on, only he remained silent, as if he needed to hear her consent for him to continue. "Go ahead, I'm listening."

This seemed to be the keywords he waited for. "It's about Gray."

Just the sound of that name changed her entire demeanor. "What about Gray? Is he all right?"

"Oh, he's fine, but…" he stopped, searching for just the right words. "He misses you terribly."

"I miss him, too," she confessed.

"He doesn't know I'm here. But I know he wants to get back with you. You're all he talks about."

"Listen, James, I appreciate you trying to play Cupid. I love Gray. I'd love to have him back. He is my husband. But I want a *man* in my life. If Gray wants to get back together, he best act like a man and tell me himself."

"I understand," James agreed, backing away slowly. "I'll talk to him."

"You do that. And you tell him what I said."

****

Weeks passed, nothing changed; Beth forgot her conversation with James. Late one night there was a knock at her door; she walked slowly to answer it. The last face she expected to see was Gray's, yet, that's who it was. She was taken so aback, she stood silently staring at him.

"Can we talk?" Gray asked softly.

Still silent, Beth moved forward, stepping out onto the porch.

"I've missed you so much," Gray said, embarrassed, looking everywhere other than at her face.

"I've missed you, too," Beth agreed, "I've never stopped loving you. But then again, I wasn't the one who walked out on our wedding night."

It was a bold and cold statement; nevertheless, it was true, and both of them knew it needed saying.

"I know what I did was wrong, and I'm willing to take it back. I want to make it right again."

"What does that mean?" she asked.

"It means I'm asking you to forgive me, and if we can try once more, to get together and try it again."

Inwardly, the prospect was like an explosion within her. She wanted so desperately to jump up and down, crying, 'Yes'. Still, there was that wise sage that lived in the back of her mind, telling her to move slowly and cautiously.

"Nothing's changed, Gray. I'm still the same woman you walked out on. I still have a past. I slept with another man before you and I had a child. You couldn't handle that."

"I've thought about it all this time. I know I was wrong. I can handle it, now."

"Tell me, Gray, why should I believe you?"

"There's no reason in the world you should believe me. But if you just give me a chance, I'll prove it to you."

"All right, I'll give you a chance to prove it. I'm willing to start over, if you are."

Gray was smiling like a schoolboy.

"Only, when I say we'll start over I don't mean from where we left off. We need to go back to the beginning, before we married. If you want my heart, you're going to have to win it all over again. Now, it's late, I'm going to bed."

"Wait," Gray pleaded. "When will I see you again?"

"You've been courting before. Let me know when and where and I'll be there."

Gray looked forlorn, that is till Beth smiled at him.

"Don't worry, Gray," she said. "If we love each other as much as we say we do, it will all work out."

****

The following weeks, Beth felt like a young girl. True to his word, Gray began to court her, just like he did when they first met. Every evening after dinner, he'd meet her on the edge of the slave quarters. They'd walk around the fields and along the edge of the forest.

Actually, it was Gray that did most of the talking. Which was just as well, Beth felt more interested in listening than speaking.

Gray was always the gentleman. When it was getting late, he'd walk her back home. It wasn't so formal that they shook hands goodnight; however, they ended their evening walks with only a nod and a smile.

They were still attracted to each other as much as ever. They could feel the tension rising, and it was sexual. They could have given in to it, after all they were married. Nonetheless, they continued keeping it platonic: Beth keeping control, observing Gray, and he keeping control because she was observing him. They both knew it had to go further, although they never spoke of it.

Gray moved closer, reaching out, taking her up in his arms. All the reasons to not go any further faded from her mind, giving in to his embrace. There lips met, deep and warm.

"Let me come in for a little while, just this once?" he asked in a whisper.

Beth smiled and nodded.

Opening the front door, she was met by an elderly woman, frail and small, smiling as she stepped onto the porch.

"Everything is just fine," said the woman. "He's asleep."

"Do you want us to walk you home?" Beth asked.

"No, dear, I'll be just fine. Goodnight." The old woman smiled at Gray as she walked passed him.

Beth stood in the doorway. "Well, are you coming in?"

Gray walked up onto the porch and into the house. "Who's asleep?" he asked.

Beth placed her index finger to her lips, warning Gray to speak lower. "Ambrose, my son," she whispered, pointing to the crib on the other end of the room, next to her bed.

Gray walked slowly across the room to the crib. He stood quietly staring down at the child for the longest time. "This is your son? But I thought..."

"He's been recently restored to me. Didn't you hear? That's all everyone's been talking about."

"I guess I don't run in those circles. Tell me, how did it happen?"

"Well, you know the story. I had a child by my old master, Collin Townsend. He sold the child from me. Just recently he's come to me saying he's found religion and he's trying to make up for all the bad he's ever done. I'd say he's making a go of it. He's brought me back my baby boy."

Gray continued to stare at Ambrose. His face was barren of all emotion, making it difficult to know what he was thinking, and clearly he was thinking.

Finally, Gray looked up at her. "You don't think folks think this is my baby, do you?"

Beth held back her laughter. "What a silly thing to ask. Of course, no one thinks that. I was never pregnant. Folks would have seen that. Besides, he's not a newborn."

"Oh, yeah, I didn't think of that," he said, lowering his eyes in shame. Then he continued. "If we ever get back together…"

"Would I keep my baby?" Beth finished the question. "Of course, I will."

Now a look of disappointment grew across Gray's face. All those old feelings of jealousy came over him, again, the ones he'd fought so hard to keep at bay. Only now, no matter how he tried to keep the thought of Collin in the back of his head, there would be his flesh and blood in their lives, pushing it to the front.

Beth was no fool. She saw the distress in his eyes.

"You know, Gray, maybe it's best you leave now. You staying the night is a big step, and I'm not sure we're ready for it. We need to keep it slow. I'm not saying we'll never, it's just perhaps some other night might be best."

Gray didn't feel like arguing. As much as he wanted Beth, there was a part of him that felt relived. Slowly, he made his way to the front door. When he opened it, moonlight flooded the room, painting everything silver. He turned to see Beth standing next to the crib.

"Beth, I…" he whimpered, unable to speak.

"We'll talk," she said, her words floating towards and passed him, escaping to the great wide open. "Tomorrow…?" she asked.

"Tomorrow," he answered, and then left.

When the door closed, the silver disappeared, and she stood in the dark. She felt like crying. They both lied. There would be no '*Tomorrow*' for them. There was a clear and possible chance they may never see each other again.

****

Beth's intuition was correct. After that night, nothing was the same. Gray never came around. Weeks went by without a word from him. He backed out of her life completely.

This saddened Beth, yet it also angered her. He filled her with such hope, and now he'd let her down, again.

All of a sudden, Collin's proposal wasn't sounding so bad or far-fetched. After all, he reunited her with Ambrose, as he'd promised. He told her that he'd turned over a new leaf, and that all she need do was give him a chance to prove it. Well, so far he'd proved it. If only she could put his moments of cruelty behind her, she could forgive and forget. She remembered what he did to Ursula. He was a murderer. As far as she knew, there might have been several more. Ursula could have been one of many.

Still, he confessed he was a sinner and had changed. Who was she to judge? Isn't it only for God to do? He was a believer, now, a new creation, if God could forgive, why not she?

However, she was still a married woman, and married women don't go off to live with other men; although, it was Gray who abandoned her, not the other way around. She felt moved to ask Reverend Gaines for his advice, except she knew what he'd say:

"Does he beat you? Does he cheat on you? Does he drink?"

Her answer to these questions could only be a resounding 'No'. Still, he'd walked out on her. The marriage was never consummated. It wasn't a real and complete marriage.

Without speaking to Reverend Gaines, directly, there was no way of knowing he would even be of that opinion. Nevertheless, it was what she told herself, which made her feel better about her decision.

At the end of one particular day, when Beth left the main house to go home, she saw a group of slaves working in the field. There was no doubt in her mind one of them was Gray.

She entered the field, walking along the newly harvested rows. When she got to the group, she approached Gray. When he looked up seeing her, the shovel fell from his hands. The others stopped working, listening.

She spoke loudly for all to hear. "Gray, I've come to tell you it's all over between us."

"Beth, can't we do this another time, when we're alone?"

"No, I want everyone to hear this. God gave folks ears to hear, so let them hear. I'm not waiting for you anymore, Gray."

"You're my wife, Beth."

"Some folks would say different. You walked out on me on our wedding night. We never consummated our marriage. That means we're not married. We never did it, Gray. Maybe, you never could? Maybe, that's why you walked out?"

She knew this not to be true. She knew the real reason he walked out that night. However, she knew she was embarrassing him, she could see it in his face. The others around giggled under their breaths. This made it worse for him, except what could he do. She was angry and wanted to hurt him. This was the best way to do it. Had she been a man, she would have punched him. This was her revenge, and it hurt him more than any punch ever could.

She had mixed feelings that night. Part of her felt pleased with how she stood up to Gray and brought him tumbling down. Another part of her felt ashamed how she acted. She had been cruel, and that wasn't like her.

She picked up Ambrose and coddled him in her arms. This took her mind off the day, putting it all behind her. It was time to move on. Her only thought now was how to get in touch with Collin and tell him she'd accept his offer.

21

Vengeance Is Mine

The moon was a thin crescent, a poor opponent for the darkness of the night. Beth's one room shack was as dim as a sealed box. It was late, she'd put Ambrose to bed hours ago. She'd just drifted off, when she woke suddenly from a heavy weight pressing down on her chest, preventing her from breathing.

It was a woman sitting squarely atop her upper body. She wasn't a heavy woman; still it was enough to keep her in check, especially with the woman's knees pressing down on Beth's shoulders. There was a sharp object pressing against her throat. Beth could only assume it was a knife.

"Where's Ambrose?" the woman snarled, pressing the blade forward, piercing the skin. Beth felt a hot trickle of blood running along the side of her throat to the back of her neck. "Where's Ambrose?" she continued. "Where's my son?" she hollered, forcing the knife further.

Fearing for her life, Beth fought back, raising her body upward, pushing the woman off her, off the bed, and onto the floor. However, in the position Beth was in, she lost her balance and fell off the bed, landing on top of the woman.

The two fought, rolling on the floor, each trying to get possession of the knife. Then the tables turned, Beth sat astride the woman's torso, her knees pinning her shoulders to the floor. Beth gained control of the knife, holding it to the woman's throat.

The dull ray of silver light coming from the crescent moon exposed the woman's face. That's when Beth recognized her.

"Fanny!" exclaimed Beth.

The woman opened her eyes. "Beth!"

The two stopped fighting, their muscles relaxed.

"Don't just sit there. I can hardly breathe. Get off me," Fanny insisted.

"Sorry," Beth replied, rolling off her, still holding the knife.

They both lay there, side by side, trying to catch their breaths.

"What is going on, Fanny?"

Fanny worked up to a sitting position. "I'm sorry, I had no idea it was you. I've been looking for Ambrose for so long. Finally, I heard he was with a woman on the Tanner Plantation. I never suspected it would be you."

Beth sat up, also. "What are you saying, Fanny, that Ambrose is your son?"

"Not long after you left the Colby Plantation, I was sold to Collin Townsend. I'd heard you were living there, only I never saw you. Collin kept me hidden most of the time. To put it nicely, I was his mistress; one of them, I imagine. When he got me in the family way, he locked me in some cabin in the woods. When I had Ambrose, he sold us both to a plantation in the next county. I figured things could be worse, so I just did my work and kept my mouth shut. One day, I come home from working in the fields to find Ambrose gone. Nobody knew anything. I went crazy. I ran away, and I've been on the run since, looking for Ambrose."

"What makes you think he's yours and not mine?" Beth questioned.

Fanny continued to describe every square inch of the boy. Most folks don't know the back of their hand as well. True, Ambrose looked a lot like Collin, only, that was understandable; after all, he was the father. And though he had many of Beth's features, looking at Fanny was like looking at Ambrose. Why had Beth not noticed it? Perhaps, she didn't want to.

Beth got to her feet and walked to the crib. Fanny rose, and stood behind her. Beth reached down, and picked up Ambrose. Slowly, the sleeping child woke and opened his eyes. Seeing Beth, he smiled. Then she turned him to face Fanny. It was like an explosion. Ambrose broke into a flood of emotion. Simultaneously, he laughed, cried, and went into a panic reaching out to his mother, Fanny.

Beth handed over Ambrose to Fanny. The two clung to each other as if their lives depended on it. For them, time stopped, the world quit spinning, at least for a moment, their moment.

Though it hurt more than a knife to her heart, Beth knew she had to step aside, and give up Ambrose to his mother, and there was no doubt in her mind Fanny was the mother.

****

A single lit candle in the center of the table illuminated the shack. Beth made some eggs, coffee, and toast. The two women sat at the table; Fanny feeding Ambrose seated on her lap.

"When did you have Ambrose?" Beth asked.

"It was in the middle of summer. Why?"

"I had a baby by Collin, too, that winter, in the same cabin, I suppose." Beth quivered, as if someone just walked over her grave. "Oh, why didn't he sell my child and not me?"

114

Fanny reached out, placing her hand on Beth's.

"I go to church regularly," said Beth. "When I didn't see you or Dahlia, I should have known something was wrong. Do you know what happed to Dahlia?"

Fanny looked as if she were about to cry. "We were both sold to Collin Townsend on the same day, and for the same reason. You know Dahlia; she'd argue with a fencepost. Every time, she'd rub him the wrong way. Finally, he got so angry with her that he beat her to death. He made me watch, so I'd stay in line. I guess it worked, because I'd do anything he told me to."

What do you say when you hear something like that? There was a long silence between them, until Beth broke it.

"I hear tell Collin found religion and turned over a new leaf," Beth added.

Fanny let out a low chuckle. "The Devil can cite Scripture for his purpose; why not Collin. Religion! The only thing he found was a way to make more money than the plantation could ever make. New leaf, my eye.... A while back this travel preacher came to the main house. Name was...?"

"Emmanuel Forrester..." Beth added.

"Yeah, that was him. He was an old friend of Collin's aunt, Mrs. Townsend. I suspect he came by to ask the old lady for a donation. He didn't know she'd passed on.

"Well, anyways, Forrester stayed for weeks. The two of them drank and womanized the entire time, hardly slept a wink. Forrester told Collin he was looking for a young buck to be part of his preaching crusades. He felt Collin had all the makings, and he was right. Collin took to it like a duck to water.

"They'd playact for hours, Forrester teaching Collin all he knew, every trick in the book. I heard it all. I'd stand out in the hall, listening to everything.

"Collin's been speaking at these rallies for a while, now, doin' real good, from what I hear, makin' money hand over fist.

"Found religion, turned over a new leaf! Why, that man is so evil, the devil's got a better chance of gettin' his soul saved than Collin."

Fanny shook her head, going silent, again, the only sound was of her scrapping the plate to get the last morsels to feed Ambrose.

Beth spoke slowly and carefully, as if she were walking through a field of snakes. "Fanny, why doesn't Ambrose speak? All this time, he never spoke a word."

"Don't you know? Couldn't you tell? Poor baby can't hear a thing," Fanny stated matter-of-factly. The way she said it clearly made it clear she didn't want to talk about it. Beth wished she hadn't asked. The weight on her heart was heavy enough, and now...

"So, what will you do next?" Beth asked.

Fanny's face went fearful, as if the question was a poison she'd tried to avoid, and now forced to swallow. "I don't know what I'll do. I can't go back. They're probably looking for me. God knows what they'll do to me, if they catch me. I'm on the run, and I guess I'll just keep runnin'."

Beth got up and walked to the stove. On a shelf on the wall was a tin container. She took it down, and dug out a handful of money from it, left of what Collin gave her. She handed the roll to Fanny.

Looking at the large amount, Fanny tried handing it back. "Beth, I couldn't..."

"Yes you can. It's not just for you; it's for Ambrose, too. Maybe, you can work your way up north."

"Maybe..." Fanny echoed sadly. "Listen, Beth, I love you, but we got to go. We need to be on our way before sunup."

"Fanny, let me hold Ambrose one last time."

She handed the child to Beth. She sat down and held the child under his arms, letting him stand on her lap. They faced each other, Ambrose smiling and cooing, Beth crying.

"Beth, we need to get goin'."

Beth reluctantly handed Ambrose to Fanny.

At the front door, they said their good-byes.

"Go north, into the woods. Stay off the roads, as best you can," Beth warned.

Fanny nodded.

"Thank you, Beth. I love you."

"I love you, too. God bless you both."

Fanny turned, scurrying off into the dark.

Beth closed the door, and leaned against it. She waited till Fanny's footsteps faded. Then she did what she had been fighting the entire night not to do, she broke down crying and fell to the floor. There she rolled about in agony. Heartbreak is far worse than anything that can happen to the body. You feel it in your soul.

****

Beth lay in her bed, unable to sleep. Her eyes were red from crying. Everything was wrong. She was totally alone in the world. She could think of no reason to live. Her father was gone; her sister was out of her life. She'd lost her child twice. Her husband abandoned her. Life had no purpose.

And then a reason for living exploded in her mind, like a lightening bolt slamming into the side of a mountain, lighting up the night sky. She'd always lived with hope, now all was hopeless. There was always love, and now all of it was taken away. Revenge would be her reason to keep breathing. All her sorrow was caused by one man, the demon better known as Collin Townsend. He was the source of her pain; she would become the cause of his. He must be stopped at all cost, by any means possible. She would make him suffer, and when she felt he'd suffered enough, she'd see that it got worse, till death was his only out.

There was a voice deep inside her telling her what she was planning was wrong. Then she took up a shovel and buried it deep within. The voice tried to tell her it was a sin against God.

"No, not a sin," she argued with her inner self. "This is what God wants, to rid the world of pestilence. Vengeance is mine saith the Lord!"

22

Trust Me

That Sunday, Beth headed to the church service with one thing in mind…to see her sister. It had been a long time since she last saw her at these services. It would be a long shot; still she felt determined. If Louise wasn't at the service, Beth would find a way to get to her, even if it meant walking onto the Colby property and hunting her down.

Luckily, when Beth entered the church and walked down the aisle, she spotted her sister sitting at the front. Louise smiled up at her, as Beth entered the pew and sat next to her. Beth was just about to say something when Pastor Gaines started the service.

Every word uttered by Pastor Gaines was wasted on Beth. She collapsed so deeply inward, she was barely aware of anything around her. She looked to her sister, lost in prayer. She seemed fine, until Beth took a closer look.

Louise's hands folded in prayer had welts on the knuckles. There were welts at the back of her neck, disappearing down her collar.

Beth placed her hand on her sister's shoulder. Louise turned to her and smiled. Then Beth lowered her hand, rubbing her sister's back. Louise's face contorted with pain. She backed away and nearly jumped to her feet. Beth stopped, and then tried to get Louise's attention. She kept her head down in prayer, and her eyes forward, seemingly afraid to look at Beth.

They remained silent till the end of the service and they were outside. Beth was set on getting to the bottom of it all. She took Louise aside.

"What's going on, Louise?"

"What are you asking?"

"You know what I'm talking about. Your hands are all bruised and there's welts going down your back."

Louise tried to walk away; Beth reached out and held her in place.

"I don't want to talk about it. Talking can only make it worse. Besides, there's nothing you can do about it."

"Yes there is," Beth replied.

Louise looked at Beth in bewilderment. "I don't understand."

"Trust me, Louise. Something is going to happen in my life, something that will give me power to help you."

"Power over General Colby…?" Louise asked, though it sounded more like a challenge than a question.

"Yes, even over General Colby. Listen to me, Louise. Have faith, and hold fast. Keep alive and well. I swear to you I'll make everything right. You'll see. Better days are ahead."

Louise wasn't sure if her sister was telling the truth or if Beth had gone mad. For both their sakes, she decided to believe in the promised deliverance.

The two sisters hugged and kissed good-bye.

Walking back to the Tanner Plantation, Beth's mind was a whirl of possibilities. She never lost the urge for revenge or hatred so strong for Collin. However, she wouldn't need to kill him, although, she wanted to be the cause. She'd ruin his life till he'd beg for death. With being Collin Townsend's mistress not only came with great responsibility, but great power, and she would wheel that power for his destruction.

If she played her cards right, she could do much good for many folks before he prayed for death.

First, she would have to gain his trust. There was only one way to do that. She would become the woman of his dreams. She'd become everything he'd ever wanted in a woman and more, and she knew what that entailed.

23

Redemption

Like magic, that night Collin appeared at Beth's front door. Let the show begin! She opened the door wearing the most welcoming smile she could muster with a hint of wantonness in her eyes. This was how she'd conduct herself around him from now on.

The first thing Collin did once he entered was to stand over the crib. He looked surprised to see it was empty.

"Where's Ambrose?" he asked, sounding confused.

Beth moved close to him, smiling up at him.

"I figured if we're going to get back together, a child would only get under foot. So, I gave him away."

Collin's face lit up with surprise and approval. He was seeing Beth in a new light and he liked what he saw, just as Beth anticipated.

Interestingly, Collin lied to Beth about her being the mother; however, the one truth to his story was that he was Ambrose's father. Yet, here he was, glad the child was out of his life.

"You should have spoken with me first. I could have got a good price for him," he said, it being his only regret.

"Would you like a drink?" she asked in a sultry voice.

He looked surprised. This was more than he could hope for. "Yes, I'd like something to drink."

She poured him a large amount of clear liquid from a jar. "All I have is moonshine. I hope you don't mind?" she said handing him the drink.

She stood by, watching him down it in a few swallows, and then she poured him another.

"What are you trying to do, get me drunk?" he asked, already his wording beginning to falter.

"That was my intention," she giggled.

This clearly was not the Beth he remembered.

So, what exactly were Beth's intentions? True, getting him drunk was part of it, although, only a small part. Of course, she planned to get him into bed, only that part would be easy. Getting her foot in the door, so to speak, would be no problem.

Her full intention was to make him want her more than any other woman. She understood he'd never be a one-woman man. Not that it mattered, nor did she care. If she could just get her hooks deep enough into him, she could fulfill her purpose and complete her destiny.

Her purpose was to get into his life and influence him. To see that he makes all the wrong moves, takes all the wrong turns, and loses everything he values in life: his property, his health, his money, and finally…his pride.

Her destiny, as far as she saw and wanted it, was to be there at the end, laughing at him as he realizes he's been duped and smiling directly into his face as he dies. Yet another thought came to her. True she'd like to see him dead. Only, death was too good for him. If she could rain down misery upon him, ruin his life, death would be a relief. No, once she got him where she wanted him, she'd pray he'd live long and suffer, and then he could die.

She tried to pour him one more glass of moonshine.

"Oh no, you don't," he said, pulling the glass from her reach.

"Just one more," she cooed. "It'll put you in the mood."

"I'm already in the mood," he laughed. "I'll tell you what; I'll have one if you have one."

She poured him another, and then one for herself. He gulped down the drink in a few fast swallows. As he did this, she took a quick sip, and then poured the rest off to the side.

Taking her in his arms, he placed his lips on hers. She was glad she had sipped some of the moonshine; it gave her a quick flash of courage, and covered up the smell of liquor on his breath.

He slowly shuffled his feet, scooting her and him across the floor to the bed. Using his weight they toppled down on the bed. His heaviness bearing down on her like dirt thrown over a grave, she could hardly breathe.

His lips to hers, he opened his mouth as if trying to devour her. His breath was hot and moist, all along her neck.

Try as much as he could, he couldn't get what he wanted, which was the feel of her skin against his. In frustration, he took hold of her clothes and tore them from her body, till she lay naked underneath him.

Using his left hand, he clumsily undressed while his right hand explored every inch of her.

Without a word or anything that resembled decent and loving human contact, Collin took her, grunting like a beast.

She could not understand how something meant to be so beautiful could be so cruel and disgusting. The image of making love with Gray on their honeymoon, an act that never happened, was all that kept her sane, although it tore into her heart like a knife.

When he finished, he rolled off her, immediately falling asleep, the liquor dictating his actions.

Feeling unclean, Beth got out of bed, walked to the other end of the shack to wash herself. Reluctantly, she returned to bed. She knew what had to be done. Collin would sleep like a bear, snoring; sounding like a hand saw sawing wood. When he woke, she would be there at his side, naked, smiling with love and contentment. She would make all his dreams come true, before starting the nightmares.

Finally, he woke, turned to smile at her; she smiled back.

"Are you hungry?" she asked.

"No, I'm fine," he answered.

"Would you like another drink?"

"Oh, no, not that," he laughed.

They lay there looking into each other's eyes, he admiring her beauty; as she held back her true feelings.

"So, when do I get to move back with you?" she asked, breaking the silence.

"Soon, my love, soon, there's one little obstacle to cross and then you can come home."

"And what is that?"

"The Tanners, they still own you. I'll just make them an offer for you."

"That might cause a problem," she replied.

"How's that…?"

"The Tanners are extremely religious folk. They won't approve. After all, I am a married woman, they know that. They know you're single, and surely they suspect your intentions. They frown on such behavior."

Collin laughed, "Don't worry, I can handle them. One thing I've learned working the preacher tours is religious folk may love God, the Bible, and such, but there's one thing many of them love even more."

"What's that?"

"Money…!"

****

"…more tea, Mr. Townsend?"

"No thank you, Mrs. Tanner. One cup is all I can tolerate when it comes to strong drink."

Mrs. Tanner tilted her head sideways, questioning. She never thought of tea as strong drink.

"Oh, and please call me Collin."

"We were close friends with your aunt. She was a good woman," Mr. Tanner said, placing his second cup of tea down, feeling uneasy about Collin's statement about strong drink.

"Thank you for saying that, Mr. Tanner. She always spoke highly of you, as well." He never really spoke about them with his aunt, as far as he could remember; nevertheless, he felt this was a good way to butter them up.

"So, Mr. Townsend, I mean Collin, to what do we owe the pleasure of your company?" Mr. Tanner asked.

"Well, I'm sure you remember me selling you a young Negress named Beth. To come right to the point: I'd like to buy her back."

"That is a strange request, in deed," Mr. Tanner said. "What is the reason for this change of heart?"

"Redemption…It has to do with my redemption."

"I don't understand," said Mr. Tanner.

"You see, I was a pagan when she was my property. I treated her badly, as I did all my slaves. This is so wrong. The Good Book says it is. I mean, they're still God's creatures. You wouldn't treat your animals the way I treated my slaves. Ever since I found religion, I've been trying to make things right." He turned to look Mrs. Tanner in the eye. "You heard me speak at the crusade, didn't you?"

"Yes, and a moving testimony it was," she admitted.

"It's all true, too. I was a heathen, fighting tooth and nail, day and night against the Lord. Now my life is different, like Zacchaeus I've decided to walk the straight and narrow. And the first person I need to settle with is Beth."

"That's very commendable," Mrs. Tanner proclaimed. "Except, there is one major problem with your plan, I don't know if you've heard. Since she's lived here she's gotten married. I would never feel good about separating a husband and wife. *What therefore God hath joined together, let not man put asunder.*"

"So true, dear lady, so true, amen and praise the Lord. Except, I've spoken with the woman in question. It seems they are no longer together. In fact, the man she married walked out on her the very night of their wedding. And here is the clincher: they never consummated the marriage. She's been living alone since."

From the looks on their faces, Collin knew he was nearly home. There was only one thing more to clinch the deal.

"Oh, did I tell you, I'm willing to pay twice what you paid for her?"

24

To Her Advantage

Beth had no problem settling back into her old room in the main house at Townsend Plantation, on the second floor, adjacent to Collin's room.

The first part of her plan was working; she was back in his life, now, to ruin it. He visited her every night in her room, or he'd call her to his. Either way, he was becoming reliant on her.

There was to be another Emmanuel Forrester crusade touring the state in a month's time. Collin received an invitation to be a part of it, appearing as the Apostle Bill. Beth thought of ways to destroy this part of his life, this moneymaking venture. Except, to do so she would have to go along on the tour, she had a month to make this happen.

One thing in her favor was Collin was not a hands-on sort of man. When his aunt was alive, he sat back and let her make all the decisions, and silently reaped all the benefits. Now that she passed on, there was no one keeping an eye on anything. He had no idea if the plantation was doing well or not, or if his overseers were doing their jobs or if they were robbing him. He never knew how much money he had in his bank account. Then again, why should he? The money the crusades were bringing in made him incredibly wealthy.

Beth would use this to her advantage. Collin gave her full reign over her spending. She could ask for any large amount of money, within reason that is, and expect to get it. As well, Collin set up a line of credit for her at nearly every shop in town. Since he was not the type to keep tabs on such matters, she could spend freely, which was what she did.

She didn't buy dresses premade. Everything was custom fitted and sown for her. Of course, each outfit needed matching jewelry. Then there were imported perfumes. She spent money freely with no regard for cost. Collin had it set up that all lines of credit were paid at the end of each month. This was all handled by his accountant and the bank. He never knew what was going out or coming in.

****

Every night they spent together. Not only did she give in to his every whim, she slowly introduced substances into their lovemaking. It became routine to have a few drinks beforehand. In time, these few drinks became a full bottle. Eventually, his drinking started early and ended late, and a number of bottles were consumed.

However, drink was only part of his upcoming habits. She began lacing his drinks with small amounts of opium powder or morphine. Also, what was all the rage at the time by those that could afford it, a few drops of chloroform on a handkerchief held under the nose produces a relaxing euphoria in the user. Beth made sure he did this in small amounts, as large amounts could lead to sudden death.

Little by little, she increased the dosages. In due course, he became addicted. He began buying his own and using on his own with no nudging needed from Beth. She too indulged now and then, yet only enough to elude any suspicion on his part.

As his habit grew, he became harder to handle. There were outbursts of anger and violence. She needed to be careful of what she said and how she acted around him. When he did hit her, she never complained nor showed any hostility. She would just bide her time. As far as she was concerned, her revenge would be in the future; however, it would be sweet.

As well, he experienced moments of paranoia. He trusted no one, and suspected everyone, from stealing from him to plotting his demise.

On the other hand, his dependence on Beth remained and grew stronger. She was the only one he trusted. She became his closest, dearest, and only friend. His one and only confidante in the world, and she was going to milk it for all its worth.

****

"When do you go off on the crusade?" Beth asked, lying naked next to Collin.

"Two weeks," he mumbled, clearly annoyed to have to answer questions.

"Two weeks? And you haven't rehearsed one speech yet," she pointed out.

He spoke in a low voice, his eyes closed. "Don't need to. I've got the knack. I just say what comes into my head. The trick is not to tell them what they need to hear, but what they want to hear."

"And what is that?" she asked.

He chuckled slightly. "What does anyone want to hear? Tell them they're loved and worthy of that love because they're special, unique and better than the others. Tell them they're God's favorite, and that good things are coming their way. Every dream will be answered, every wish will be granted. All the aches and pains will fade. Those money worries will be a thing of the past. Because God wants you healthy, happy, and rich, bad things only happen to those other people, the ones without any faith. All this can be yours. All you have to do is clap you hands three times, spin in a circle while you whistle Dixie, stop and spit. Of course, faith wouldn't hurt…faith in God and in me. And the test of that faith is how much of a donation you put in the basket when it comes around. Remember, you will receive one hundredfold. A dollar will get you a hundred, and so on. Just imagine the possibilities."

"You really do have this down, don't you?" she cooed.

"Stick with me and you'll learn something," he replied.

"Stick with you," she echoed. "That's what I wanted to talk to you about."

"What now?" he moaned, knowing that tone in her voice always indicated that she wanted something.

Beth moved closer to him, resting her head on his chest. Her voice became a cat's purr. "I was hoping I could go with you on the crusade."

"Don't even think about it," he replied.

"But I'll be here alone, missing you."

This caused him to open his eyes. "What do you really want?"

"I'll be bored here without you. It'll be fun. I can pretend I'm your servant. I can take care of everything for you. I'll take care of your clothes, I'll see to your meals. You won't have to lift a finger."

"No!" His voice grew firm.

She began petting the length of him with one hand. "And at night, I'll wash you and take away all the stress of the day." She continued stroking him till she could feel his blood rising. "Come on, Collin, it'll be fun."

He rolled over on top of her.

"Please, Collin, you know how happy I can make you."

He nuzzled into her neck. "Very well, you can come. Only, one mistake and your on the train home."

"You won't regret it. You'll see."

25

I Have my Reasons

Noah Hancock was the head overseer on the Townsend Plantation longer than anyone could remember or who preceded him. He was a slender elderly man with steel gray hair and eyes, wearing faded overalls that knew their way to work as well as he, after many years of wear and tear on the job. He was the darkest white man you could imagine, his skin tanned by summer after summer spent under the sun.

It was the end to a long day. Hancock stood on the loading dock, as Chester Grimmer and one of his men pulled the back of his wagon up to the dock. Together they would weigh the daily harvest at the Townsend Plantation. Grimmer would load his wagon with the cotton and pay for it in cash. As always, Hancock made out a sales slip for the transaction. The next day he'd ride into town and deposit the amount. The deposit slip and then sales slip were submitted to the accountant. This was how it went every week, and to anyone who didn't know better, it all seemed on the up and up.

Hancock rolled his eyes in disgust when Beth drove her carriage up to the loading dock. Only, he knew better. This was the boss's mistress, he needed to treat her like a queen, which he did.

"Good afternoon, ma'am, how may I help you?" he asked, smiling down from the dock. It was clearly a forced smile, looking nearly perfect save for the three missing teeth in the front.

"Mr. Hancock, I need to speak with you. Could we talk in your office?"

"Yes, ma'am," he sang. He pointed to a full sack of cotton. "I got this one last load to weigh and then I can send Mr. Grimmer on his way."

"Tell Mr. Grimmer I'd like to speak with him, too."

"Yes, ma'am," he answered, the singsong in his voice replaced by a tone of trepidation.

One of the men helped her down and took charge of the carriage and horse. She entered Hancock's office and sat before his desk, waiting.

A moment later, Hancock entered, and stood behind his desk, Grimmer at his side. "So, how could we be of service?" His speech suggested he didn't have time for what he viewed as 'This nonsense'.

"Sirs, I'm sure you both know who I am. Technically and legally, I'm not Collin Townsend's wife, I'm his mistress, but for all intents and purposes I am his wife. Let's just say I have the man's ear.

"Now, you two gentlemen seem industrious and smart." It wasn't hard to tell she spoke with her tongue in cheek. "It wouldn't surprise me that, just now and then, that is, now and then the two of you skim a little off the top."

"Well, I never…!" Mr. Grimmer growled, giving the impression he was about to walk out.

"Never, Mr. Grimmer…? I have it on high authority that you do, and I can prove it." This being one of many of Beth's lies, still, who could recant it?

Mr. Hancock's approach was far different. He played his cards close, but he was willing to play.

"What are you drivin' at, ma'am? Are you tryin' to blackmail us into givin' you a piece?"

"Not blackmail, sir. I'm suggesting a partnership, where we steal five times more than you two could ever dream of stealing."

"And how do you propose that?" Grimmer asked.

"We fix the scales to read twenty percent less," she replied.

Both men began laughing loudly.

"You must think us pretty stupid, don't you? You imagine we didn't think of that?" Hancock said, trying not to choke on his words. "There's only one major problem with that. Once a month if not two or three times, Master Townsend shows up with his weights to check the scales. We never know when he'll pop up and give us the once over. If he knew we were doin' false weights, we'd not only be out of a job, we'd be arrested. It wouldn't surprise me if they hanged us."

The two men fell back into their laughter.

"I understand the situation; and I have a solution," she said.

The laughter ended as quickly as it started. She waited till she had their full attention, smiling like the cat that ate the canary.

"You see, gentlemen, I know where Master Townsend keeps those weights and I have access to them. I also know of a blacksmith that is willing to make exact copies, only these weights will be hollow within – twenty percent worth."

The two men stood dumbfounded.

"And what do you want for you hand in this?" Hancock finally asked.

"One percent…"

"One percent…?" he laughed. "That sounds like a mighty low amount, wouldn't ya say?"

"For some," she replied. "I have my reasons. One percent will suit me just fine."

"How do we know we can trust you?" Grimmer asked.

"You can't know. I could say the same thing about you two. We're just going to have to crawl out on the limb together and see if it will hold us. That reminds me. While we're out on that limb, let's not get greedy. We can make a lot of money for an awfully long time if we keep our eyes smaller than our stomachs."

Beth rose from her chair, started for the door, stopping when she thought of a few more items

"Oh yes, the blacksmith that I spoke about, he's asking for one hundred dollars to make the duplicate weights. Of course, we'll need a matching set for here. That would make it two hundred dollars. Not only would I like you two gentlemen to pay for it, I need it right now, before I leave."

"Two hundred dollars, on the expensive side, I'd say," Grimmer moaned.

"Not really," Beth smiled. "I'd call it a bargain. How much would you charge to break the law, and that is what he'll be doing, knowing if he's caught he'll lose everything. No, Mr. Grimmer, I think it quite reasonable and well worth it."

Hancock reached down to the lowest draw of his desk, bringing up a cash box, and laying it down. Once he unlocked the box, he reached in, pulling out a wad of bills, he counted out two hundred dollars.

"Here ya are, ma'am. Would you like a receipt for that?" he asked jokingly, wearing a self-assured smile.

"That's very funny," she replied. "No, if anybody asks, I was never here."

The two men smiled knowingly.

Beth placed her hand on the door, and turned to make one last point.

"One other thing, don't either of you try to back stab me. I'll uncover this entire mess to the authorities faster than you can say Jack Robinson. Oh, and if I'm found dead, everything we've talked about today is in a well hidden letter."

Not knowing how much was the truth and how much was a bluff, the two men decided it best to play it on the up and up with her.

"Good day, gentlemen," she sang out as she slammed the door.

26

Damned If I Do

"There's a Colored woman out here to see you, sir."

Kent Martin looked up from his desk in bewilderment. "Why would you bother me with something like that? Send her away."

"She says she's from the Townsend Plantation. She told me her name is Beth Hanley and she's Collin Townsend's mistress."

Martin dropped his pen and burst into laughter. "She said that to you?"

"She did, sir, in those exact words without as much as a blink."

Still laughing, Martin leaned back in his chair. "Show her in. This promises to be worth a listen."

Kent Martin looked far too young to be so well established, and he was, with his dark slicked down hair and well trimmed beard. He dressed like a banker, knowing it made clients feel secure. He never married and planned to stay that way. His philosophy being: *Why buy the cow, when you can get the milk free.*

Fittingly, his office was across the street from the bank. His grandfather started the business, and then willed it to his son, Kent's father, who willed it to Kent. It was three generations of scoundrels.

Beth dressed stylish for the occasion. When the clerk closed the door behind him, she stepped forward. "Mr. Martin, we finally meet."

"My clerk tells me you describe yourself as Collin Townsend's mistress. That's a bold introduction, if I ever heard one. So, what brings you here, today?"

Without an invitation, Beth took a seat in front of his desk; she smiled boldly at him.

"Let's not play games, Mr. Martin. You know exactly who I am. You're Mr. Townsend's accountant, taking care of most of his financial transactions. So, you know who I am and how much of his money I spend every month. After all, you see and pay his bills for him."

The smile left Martin's face.

"What I'd like to know is why you're doing such a poor job of it. You see how much I spend each month; yet, you've never warned Collin about it.

"I thought about this. Why wouldn't you? Then it dawned on me. You don't want Collin or anybody else poking around. That means you've got something to hide."

The smile returned to Martin's face.

"Seemingly we're at a standoff. Very well, let's just say I am taking advantage of the situation; of course, I wouldn't want anyone looking at the books. Likewise, you don't want to be found out. So, what is your point? Why are you here?"

"Why...I'm here to help you, Mr. Martin. I know you're a crook. Your only fault is you think small, so, you steal small. I'm here to help you get over that. I'm here to make more money for you and me."

"Go ahead, I'm listening."

"We both know how I enjoy shopping. What Collin doesn't know won't hurt him...to a great extent. As much as I appreciate expensive things, it doesn't put food on the table or money in my pocket. All the shops have a return policy. I could return the items for cash. The problem with that is the store sends a return statement to his accountant, that being you."

"I think I see where you're going with this," he laughed softly. "Please, continue."

"When I return an item, and receive cash, and you don't register the return receipt, we could split the money."

Martin leaned forward. "You realize if I accept your offer it's the same as admitting I'm a thief."

"True, but no one has to know. It will by our little secret. Besides, if you don't take my offer, I'll expose you for what you are. You'd be wise to partner up with me."

"Damned if I do, and damned if I don't," he said, smiling.

"Exactly...!"

27

As Predictable as the Weather

There are many rules to being a successful mistress:

Never show your true intelligence to your man, especially if you outshine him. All good ideas are from him, all failing ideas are yours, or better, someone else's. If you can't handle that, don't even start.

Whatever he says goes. Save for something that might get you killed, there is no suspected sexual position or action not considered. And remember you are always in the mood. Even when your head is splitting wide open with pain, grit your teeth and get through it.

There's no reason to get Biblical about it. You don't have to carve graven imagines of your master, fall to your knees and proclaim false and unholy idolatry. But lifting him up high above all others is certainty. Just give him what he wants when he wants it.

Always keep in mind your master is a narcissist, pagan, egomaniac, and probably a libertine. The pursuit of his pleasure comes first, the happiness of others is unnecessary and not worthy of consideration. Don't expect him to be a one-woman-man, it's not going to happen. Your best strategy is to embrace it. Make sure there are many women in his life and bed; only be sure their talents fall short of yours. You must remain the center of his attention. You may even want to join in, play a part in it, and show how much of a true partner you are. You must declare his happiness as pinnacle, far above that of others, and especially your own. You find your joy in making him happy; at least make him believe that. This will cause a bond between the two of you that no man could break asunder.

However, the most important thing to being a gentleman's mistress is to never act like a wife. Even the slightest resemblance could send you packing, sold to another plantation with the possibility of fieldwork, which means long hours of back breaking labor, ending in a depressing and shorter life.

So, to make things happen, it's always best to give the impression the idea was his. In the case of Collin Townsend this was easy. His journey into drink and drugs quite often left him with memory lapses, which he expected Beth to fill in.

On a few occasions, she expressed her concern for her sister's welfare, asking him to buy her, and to see that she went to a better plantation than the Colby Plantation. However,

Collin saw it as an opportunity to add another woman in his life. That was not Beth's intention.

"I appreciate what you're trying to do," she told him one evening over dinner. "I just think my sister and I living in the same house, serving the same man, would be a nightmare."

Being intoxicated, the tête-à-tête passed in a blur with him often getting lost in the details. To save face, he continued the conversation, as if he knew what she was talking about.

"So what would you have me do?" he asked.

"It pains me to think of my sweet sister in the hands of that brute, General Colby, she'd be far better off on the Tanner Plantation. You need to buy her from Colby and give her to the Tanners."

"And pray tell, my dear, why would I do such a non-profitable act of stupidity?"

"Are you going to go back on your word to me," she hollered. "You asked me what I wanted for my birthday, and I told you I wanted my sister safe from that animal, Colby. You're not going to go back on your promise?"

Of course, she was repeating a promise that was never made from a conversation that never happened. Beth played it well, putting Collin on the spot, making it sound like it was all his idea.

Again, wanting to save face he announced, "Very well, I'll go see Colby, tomorrow."

****

The next day in true Collin fashion, he forgot all about it. Cautiously, she reminded him, still nothing. It wasn't till after three days of reminding him that Collin visited General Colby.

Beth asked about the results of the meeting. "So, what did he say?"

"He said he's having too much fun with her to want to sell her."

Beth was afraid of that.

"How much did you offer him?"

"I offered him one hundred; he just laughed and shook his head."

"One hundred…is that all? My birthday present and all you're willing to spend is one hundred?"

Collin's face turned red with anger, he rose from his seat and walked away. "You know, Beth, little by little you're starting to sound like a wife!"

Beth shook her head, disgusted with herself. She was walking on thin ice; and she was the one who put herself there.

General Colby stood on his porch, watching a carriage drive onto his property. He smiled, as he the carriage came closer and he recognized the driver.

When Beth pulled up in front of him, he began to laugh. "I never thought I'd see you again. You're either the bravest or the most stupid person I know. You realize just by coming onto my property you're breaking the law, and I could have you shot."

"Then you wouldn't get to hear the offer I've come to make you. Now, *that* would be stupid."

"I suspect this has to do with your sister. Collin Townsend was here the other day and made me an insulting offer for her. . . .twenty dollars. . .indeed."

The words twenty dollars echoed in her mind, another reason to distrust and hate Collin Townsend.

Beth's first impulse was to start a bidding war with Colby. After all, any amount over twenty dollars was an improvement. However, when it came to the freedom of her sister, Beth didn't want to take any chances. She decided to lay all her cards on the table.

"I'll give you one thousand dollars, cash, right now."

"I'm impressed. It seems you've done well for yourself."

"Then it's a deal?" she asked.

"Yes, it's a deal."

Beth took out a bundle of cash, handing it to Colby. He stuffed it in his top pocket.

"Aren't you going to count it?"

"No, I consider myself a good judge of character. I'd wager it's all there."

Beth got back up onto the wagon. "I want you to deliver my sister to Mr. and Mrs. Tanner, within the hour."

"What am I suppose to say to them, when they ask me why I'm delivering a slave girl free of charge?"

"Tell them she's a gift from Collin Townsend, to make up for taking me away. She's to have my old shack to live in and my old job. Not having to pay for any of this, I assume you'll have no trouble with the Tanners."

"Seems you know the Tanners as well as I do," he laughed.

"Oh, and one last thing, General. . ."

He looked at her, giving his full attention.

"Don't you dare double-cross me or I swear I'll kill you."

Again, he laughed. "I wouldn't think of it. Like I said, I'm a good judge of character. I know you would."

The seasons were shifting, the evenings were changing. Where you could once harvest till eight o'clock, now, it was too dark to see your hand in front of your face at seven.

Gray worked till six in the evening when it was nearly too dark to find your way.

"Gray, I need to talk with you," a mysterious voice called out from behind a bush. With little light, the figure of a woman stepped out, Gray recognized her.

"Beth! It's you! You've come back," he shouted for a moment.

"No, Gray. I haven't come back to you. I need to ask a favor."

"You're my wife; you need to be with me."

"No, Gray, this hasn't been a marriage since the preacher told us to say *I do*. I've made some deals around town. My sister, Louise, is living here on the Tanner Plantation. I arranged for her to stay where I used to live and to do my old job. She'll be new here. She's young and innocent and she's beautiful. It's going to be hard for her. What I'd like you to do is watch over her, you and your brothers James and Victor."

Then she thought about the incident with Victor.

"Well, maybe not so much Victor," she added.

Beth started backing away into the darkness, like a ghost fades into the mist.

"Will we ever get back together?" Gray asked.

"I couldn't say, Gray. At this point, I'd say no, probably never. Then again, I've lived on this earth long enough to never trust the word never."

"Will I at least see you, again?"

Beth laughed. "It's a small world; it wouldn't surprise me."

Beth backed up so deeply into the dark, she was hardly visible.

"You're a good man, Gray. You got a few rough edges that'll smooth out in time. You'd be a good choice for my sister, Louise."

"If you remember correctly, Beth, I'm still a married man."

"Well, there's not many who'd argue the point for our marriage; you and I never consummating and all, if you remember?"

"Is that what makes a marriage?" Gray argued.

"It does to some," replied Beth. She continued, "Besides, we only married till death do us part."

"What's that supposed to mean?"

"It means what it means. Life is as predictable as the weather."

28

Hallelujahs and Hosannas

The similarities between a religious crusade and a circus are many. Some may say to compare them is sacrilegious, which maybe so with a genuine crusade with legitimate preachers. However, the Emmanuel Forrester Crusade was never sanctioned by any religious institution or denomination. Emmanuel Forrester was a self-proclaimed preacher, prophet, healer, and holy man. If truth be known, his crusade was a circus. Its main object was to make money, always through trickery. In its own right, a form of entertainment giving people what they want, tickling their ears, and giving false hope. The one major difference between Forrester's Crusade and a circus is a circus is what it is, everything is up front, take it or leave it, whereas, Forrester's Crusade was covered in deceit.

They gathered at the train station. The entire train was designated to the crusade. The equipment, the workers, took up most of the train. Speakers, like Collin, received private compartments. Emmanuel Forrester housed in a full private car at the tail end.

The crusade was to last for two full months on the road. Beth couldn't help smiling, thinking about all the havoc Noah Hancock, the overseer, and Kent Martin, the accountant, would shower down on the Townsend Plantation. As the old saying goes: *When the cat's away . . .*

When they pulled into a town, it was organized chaos. The workers spent the night setting up the tents, the chairs, and such. Meanwhile, Forrester and the other speakers lodged at whatever was the finest hotel in the town.

It was during the first hotel stay that Beth began learning what a façade the Forrester Crusade wore. Besides Forrester, and Collin who went by the name of The Apostle Bill, there were two other speakers. There was Calvin Eastman; he was presented as the wise old owl, with words of wisdom. Most of those words were praise for Forrester.

Beth began understanding that as good as these speakers were no one was allowed to outshine Forrester, and to promote him whenever possible. In fact, the other speakers were nothing but warm up acts for his grand performance.

The fourth speaker was Quentin Rollins, the exact opposite of Eastman. He was the young, innocent lamb who begged you to journey with him down the road of salvation. Of course, what waited at the end of that road was Emmanuel Forrester.

It goes without mentioning, Sister Sara would be there with her angelic looks and voice. She kept the mood going between the speakers. She kept the people up and hopeful. Her voice moved all to tears, keeping them in an emotional state.

Everyone had their own room, save for Forrester who had his own suite. Beth realized that no one traveled alone. Everyone had a traveling companion, to put it in respectable terms. Of course, Beth was with Collin. The others had their mistresses, too, including Sister Sara.

Always in the public eye and examined more closely by the world, especially in newspapers. Forrester traveled with a young beautiful woman, which he introduced to all as his daughter. It was well known Forrester was a widower and the young lady's only protection in this cruel world, so he took her with him everywhere he went. Her room connected to his suite.

Later, Beth learned the girl was sixteen years old. Her name was Rosalinda Kerry. She came from a poor family living in the Appalachians. She ran away from home when she was fourteen, turning to prostitution to stay alive. Forrester met her at a cathouse he frequented and took a liking to her. She jumped at his offer to be his mistress, hidden behind the mask of a daughter. After all, it was an easier life to please one old man five times each week than five old men every night, seven nights each week. The money was far better, not to mention the additional benefits.

That evening, all the speakers and their companions nestled into a private room for dinner. It was then Beth got a clear understanding what sort of people she was dealing with. Let's just say Collin fit in like a hand in a glove, for they were all like him, if not worse.

Interesting to note, though drink and drugs was plentiful within the small group, Collin's addiction was far more noticeable. Beth did her job well. Though none of the others cared, Forrester noticed and worried. His tight little caravan of libertines made good money; only, everything needed to be kept hush-hush. As far as the outside world knew, they were a traveling group of God's chosen. It was their first get together, a time for revelry and carousing. He'd not mention it. However, from then on, he would keep a close eye on Collin. The chain could not afford a weak link.

Forrester's reaction to Collin did not go unnoticed by Beth. Sensing what occurred, she knew one of her main endeavors would be to keep Collin intoxicated.

Despite all the levity, they called it an early night, each going to their room. It would be a long and taxing day tomorrow. They needed to be at peak performance. True, they were all liars and thieves; still, they were professional liars and thieves.

****

The next morning before sunrise, everyone was under the big top. The workers tied all the loose ends, making all the last minute adjustments. The musicians rehearsed, as did the singers lead by Sister Sara. The speakers were prepped and ready, their companions, domestic partners, backstage.

Finally, they did a run-through, without the full speeches. This was when Beth learned the great secret of the Emmanuel Forrester Crusade.

They called them *The Freaks*. Not sideshow freaks, mind you, no, these were folks with special talents, showmen and women in their own right. There leader was a man named Jarvis Kensington. A white man somewhere in his late forties or early fifties, a most unremarkable looking man, as easy to forget as any stranger you pass on the street. Although, he was strong and flexible, he wore clothes that covered his muscular physic. However, his true beauty was his mind. He could make any audience believe he was the saddest of God's creatures, worthy of all pity, and in need of a miracle. And when it came to miracles he could deliver.

The rest of those in his troop were actors, folks that could make you believe they were deaf, blind, or crippled. Two of them were contortionists, able to twist their bodies into unhuman shapes that made young women scream, old women cry, and men moved to sympathy, mercy, and compassion.

Jarvis worked up a new scam especially for that day. He and Forrester got in place to rehearse it, Forrester onstage and Jarvis at the tent's entrance. Beth stood on the side of the stage. Her curiosity got the best of her, she had to watch.

"I feel the spirit descending upon us. If anyone needs healing, let them come forward."

That was Jarvis' cue. A loud scream came from the back of the tent, sounding like an animal in pain, caught in a trap.

Two men guided Jarvis up the main aisle to the stage. The hair on the back of Beth's neck stood on edge. It was one of the most frightening sights she'd ever seen. His eyes, that's what was so remarkable. Jarvis' eyes were just white orbs with no pupils, just solid globes of white.

Beth knew it was a trick, but her mind could not fathom how he achieved the illusion, that is if it was an illusion, it looked so real.

The two men guided Jarvis unto the stage. At center stage, Forrester took hold of Jarvis, turning him around to face the audience. Of course there was no audience, this being a rehearsal. He placed his hands on Jarvis' shoulders, pressing him down onto his knees.

Forrester spoke loud and with power, the power most folks only expect to come from God.

"How long have you been like this, sir?" Forrester asked in a shout.

"All my life, sir…"

"Do you believe the Lord can give you sight?"

"Yes, I do!"

"Then your faith has healed you! In the name of the Holy God, I command you to see!"

Jarvis let out another howl of pain; he bent over placing his face into his hands, crying and moaning. Then he raised his head, moving his hands aside. His eyes were as right as yours or mine with deep brown color.

"I can see! I can see! Lord God almighty, I can see!"

Tears flowed from his new made eyes. Forrester helped him to his feet.

"How many fingers am I holding up?" asked Forrester.

"Three," Jarvis replied.

"And now how many?"

"Five."

"Praise the Lord, the man is healed. Go, my son, and sin no more."

This statement was blasphemy in itself; however, the people watching loved it.

Jarvis began to walk away when Forrester grabbed him, holding him center stage.

Forrester called out in a loud voice. "Now that his eyes are well, maybe the Lord will do something about his nose, because he sure smells bad."

The joke was too much for Jarvis to keep in character. The two men burst into laughter, falling into each other's arms.

"It's a fabulous illusion, Jarvis. You're a genius! We'll use it in today's show," Forrester proclaimed.

Jarvis broke free from Forrester and started towards the back of the stage. He passed Beth. She reached out to him.

"How did you do that?" she asked.

"Simple," he said, digging into his pocket, pulling out two halves of a chicken's eggshell.

"You wore chicken eggshells?" she asked, sounding amazed.

"Only a half shell on each eye. It's extremely uncomfortable, and you gotta be careful not to cut yourself, still, it gets the job done."

"It sure does," she nearly cheered. "You scared the bejeezus out of me. What I don't understand is how you got them off."

"It's simple. When I'm bent over cryin' with my hands over my face, I take them out. When I rise to my feet, I place the shells in my pockets."

"It looked so real," Beth exclaimed.

"Yeah, people see what they wanna see."

****

After the run-through, all the main performers went back to the hotel to their rooms to rest. This was when Beth did the most damage. She started by offering Collin a small brandy. He never could turn down brandy. Besides, it was only a small one. What harm could it do?

The fact was Collin could no longer stop at one small drink. It always lead to another small drink, and then a larger one, and then another. Beth trained him well; however, she wasn't going to leave it at that. A few grains of opium laced the drinks, as well as a few inhales of chloroform adding to the effect. Eventually, Collin passed out on the bed. She'd let him sleep up till the last minute.

When it was time for the performers, to return to the site, Beth shook Collin awake. He woke with a start, clearly disorientated. It took two of the strongest men to get him downstairs and into the carriage. All the while, this was done under the watchful eye of Forrester. Such behavior worried him. He spoke with Collin about this, backstage.

"I understand, Collin. I like a good time as much as the next person But there's a time and place for everything under the sun, and now is not the time. This is your first and last warning. I won't tolerate such behavior. Keep this up and you're out. Now, I was going to put you on first; only, I'll put you on just before me. That'll give you time to sober up." He looked to Beth. "Walk him around to get his head clear." He turned again to Collin. "Smarten up, Collin." Then he walked away.

Beth placed Collin's arm around her shoulder, and began to walk him in a circle in the area behind the stage.

She coaxed him along, "That's right, one foot in front of the other."

"Oh, Beth, you're so good to me. What would I ever do without you?"

"Curl up and die, I suppose."

****

Just when you thought you knew every scheme the Forrester Crusade used to separate folks from their money, there was another waiting right behind it. As she learned of these things, little by little, Beth became jaded; nothing surprised her anymore.

This swindle was so simple, it was undetectable. It was called *Forrester's Prayer Warriors* or *Prayer Team*. As the audience waited in line to enter the main tent, they were given small cards and pencils. They were asked to write down their names, addresses, and what were their ailments or problems they wanted God to intervene. They were told that all cards would be put in piles, and Forrester's Prayer Warriors would pray over the requests. The fact that this was offered at no cost, everyone filled out their card.

Once the audience was seated, they delivered the cards backstage to Forrester. He and two of his staff weeded through the stacks, looking for the ones with the most potential. The ones they felt were of no importance they trashed. With that done, Forrester proceeded over the next two hours to memorize them for later use.

The tent was full; the folks cheered, sang along, cried, prayed, and pleaded for help. There were some so moved by the experience, they fell to their knees. Others to the ground where they rolled about with their eyes closed in ecstasy, while others stood on their chairs howling the way dogs do at a full moon. It was complete and utter chaos, yet well controlled by Forrester's people.

The day was going smoothly with no surprises, the music, the singers, the speakers, all went as planned. To Beth's surprise and dismay, Collin sobered up before his time to speak came up. The Apostle Bill was all anyone could hope for. He was witty, smart, and heart moving. When he left the stage to the cheers of the audience, he was all smiles. Though disappointed, it didn't alarm Beth, she would only have to try harder, and she'd have plenty of time to do so; this was only the first day of the crusade.

When Forrester hit the stage, it was as if the heavens opened, raining joy and love on all.

He preached a little, not too much, people don't want their ears banged; they want them tickled. Mostly, they wanted to be wowed.

Remembering the cards, he called out names, addresses, ailments, and prayerful questions and needs. He prayed over them, he laid hands on them. They cried, howled, swooned to the ground, and then rose with their hands held high to hallelujahs and hosannas, claiming to be healed.

Then came his hired actors, The Freaks; there were double-jointed contortionists, their twisted bodies made straight. Cripples tossed aside their canes and crutches. Then, Jarvis with his pupil-less eyes was guided to the stage, and then the miraculous appearance of his brown eyes, the entire crowd fell to their knees. Understandably, this was the best time to ask for donations.

As Sister Sara sang, tearing at everyone's heartstrings, workers passed baskets around for the collection. More than once they had to stop to empty them, and then continue the harvest.

There was a time when Forrester would position himself at the mouth of the tent, shaking hands and wishing them all the best, as they left. He figured the personal touch was good for business, and it was. However, this took hours. Everyone wanted a piece of him. Each and every one of them had a need or at least a story to tell.

Now, before the last note from the orchestra and singers sounded, Forrester and his colleges were in carriages on their way to the hotel.

This particular night, Collin and Beth wound up in the same carriage as Forrester and his so-called daughter, Rosalinda. Forrester was in a good mood, smiling. He spoke directly to Collin.

"Sorry about the reprimand earlier, old man. You have to understand, I run a tight ship here, no slipups. It was a long hard road getting to where I am today, and I'll not give it up. I can be your friend, but I swear the first person to try to ruin it, I personally will throw to the lions."

The seriousness left his voice. He looked out the window of the carriage. He could see the tent off in the distance, the audience exiting. It pleased him to admire his handiwork.

"I love this, I really do," he said softly. "Don't get me wrong, the money is good, and I do enjoy it. Only, I enjoy the hoopla of it all. If I had to, I think I'd do it for nothing." He turned, smiling at the others around him. "Thank God, we don't have to," he laughed.

29

Out on His Ear

The crusade remained in each city for two days. That was enough time to bleed the community dry, not as much as a penny left.

Beth did her best to keep Collin happy and, of course, drunk. Still, he was able to get through his performances. Nevertheless, Forrester on no account took his eyes off Collin, unable to trust him as far as he could throw him.

To Beth's surprise and delight, Collin took up a new vice. This he did on his own with no coaxing from her. As busy and demanding as their careers were, there was still long hours of free time when there was nothing to do but sit and wait. To pass the time, often there was a card game, somewhere.

Collin took to gambling like someone born for it, as they say. Only gambling was a cruel mistress. It took him for every cent he had till once again he wired his bank for more money. His drunkenness that Beth encouraged kept his head foggy and only able to make poor decisions, thus making him a poor gambler.

This caused Beth to change her strategy. The longer they remained on the road with the crusade the more Collin destroyed his life. Not to mention the devastation happening back at the plantation and the accountant's office.

She racked her mind, coming up with different scenarios to get Collin fired from the crusade, only, now it was best to see it through to the end.

She made sure he remained strong in his addictions, except, now, she needed to space his indulgences carefully. Often, she'd lace his whiskey with great amounts of opium powder early in the day, this would make him sleep. When he awoke, though drossy, he was still able to hit the stage with full force. After each performance, she would be sure to get him drinking again. This would keep him out of sorts for gambling throughout the night.

No, she would not kill Collin, though she believed him to be her greatest enemy and worthy of death. She would bring him to the edge of the cliff where he would wish for death, look down at the abyss and think it better than life.

****

It was the last week of the crusade, time for Beth to make her move.

Amidst all happening in and around Collin's life, one thing never faltered, his roving eye for the women. For his sake, it was a good thing he'd taken Beth along. For although he treated his speakers and their companions like kings and queens, Forrester kept them separated from the world. One inappropriate word, look, or encounter with one of the audience and his entire empire would collapse.

Understand, even though these gatherings were of a religious nature, it did not stop some of the admirers to lust after these men. If that sounds too absurd and inconvincible, then bless you, for you are not fully of this world, still innocent and naïve.

However, for the rest of us sinners, still entangled with matters of the flesh, we understand how easy one falls.

For this reason, Forrester sheltered his orators. Interesting to note, this veil of separation and mystery made them all the more alluring.

Since there was no touching, only looking, Collin did as much looking as a man with two eyes could. Collin, like so many other men, thought of himself as a king bee and all women flowers, and in this garden it was his duty to pollinate as many flowers as possible.

Knowing this, Beth decided to use this to her advantage. She did this with the help of a fellow conspirator; of all people, Rosalinda, Forrester's traveling companion and imitation daughter.

It wasn't an immediate collaboration; friendships take time to form. Night after night, slowly, Beth weaseled her way into Rosalinda's confidence till they were good friends, willing to bear their souls to each other.

Rosalinda's story was as expected. Born to a poor Appalachian family, she ran away from home at an early age, not to the dismay of her family, one less mouth to feed was a blessing.

On her own, she found the only way to keep the wolf from the door and her belly full was to work the cathouses. After all, she had no skills to mention, save for her beauty. It wasn't a good life but it was her life.

Then everything changed, Forrester discovered her and was enthralled. He set it up for her to travel as his daughter by day, and his concubine by night. He was a demanding lover, although because of his age it was not often. This made for a good life for Rosalinda, finally.

It didn't take Beth long to learn what Rosalinda's greatest motivation in life was – money. She examined Beth's proposal with few questions, liking the answers, and immediately accepted.

"Is Forrester jealous of you?" Beth asked.

Rosalinda laughed. "Jealous? If a man so much as looks at me wrong he'd kill him. Only, because of his age and status in life, he wouldn't do it himself; he'd hire someone else to do it."

This sounded good to Beth. She made her proposal.

"If I were to pay you, could you make Forrester believe Collin approached you, nearly raping you?"

"Pay me!" Her eyes lit up. "How much would you pay me?"

"One hundred dollars," smiled Beth.

Rosalinda smiled back. "I can make Forrester believe anything. For one hundred dollars I could convince him that Collin treated me like his own and deserves to be kicked off the roster and never used again. That is what you're trying to achieve here, isn't it?"

Beth just smiled. She reached into her deep pockets and came up with a clump of money, handing over one hundred dollars.

Rosalinda took the money, placing it to the bottom of her deep pockets. "Prepare to be astonished. When I'm finished you'll want to applaud, please don't."

With that Rosalinda marched down the hall till she stood before Forrester's room. She reached up taking hold of the shoulder of her blouse. She pulled on it, ripping it, exposing her shoulder, chest, and breast. Then she pounded on the door.

"Daddy…Daddy…open up, I need your help." She cried through the door.

When it opened, Forrester saw her predicament. In shock, he took hold of her by the arms. Not wanting a scene, he pulled her into his room, slamming the door closed.

Beth rushed down the hall, placing her ear to Forrester's door.

"Oh, Daddy…Daddy…I'm so frightened, you've got to help me."

Beth understood why she called him 'Daddy', in public. To call him 'Daddy" in private was some kind of pleasure ride only the two of them were on.

"What has happened, dear?"

"It's that fiend, Collin Townsend; he's been ogling me for weeks. Finally, he got hold of me. I told him I belong to you, it didn't matter. I don't know how, but I got away and here I am."

Forrester did not do his own dirty work; he sent two of his goons to Collin's room. Beth sat up in bed, wide eyed as if surprised, the blanket covering her modesty.

Within the hour, Collin was no longer part of the caravan. He was out on his ear, to put it mildly.

Beth gave Collin a drink laced with opium to calm him down. He fell asleep in seconds. Tomorrow would be a time for new plans.

30

Bad to Worse

During the train ride home, Collin silently stared out the window, wondering what went wrong. He never learned the reason, just orders to leave. When he demanded to speak with Forrester, two ruffians simply pushed him aside. When he pleaded to see Forrester, he was laughed at and told to leave. He never knew the accusations of Rosalinda. Never able to make his case, he left sad and bewildered.

Beth did and said everything she could to console him. Their relationship was changing, the bond growing stronger. In the bedroom little altered, yet, in conversation and outside the bedroom, he became more reliant on her. She was his lifeline, his confidant and only friend. As for his dependence on her, there are small children more independent of their mothers. Beth was becoming his entire world.

The moment the carriage rode onto the property, both Collin and Beth sensed something was wrong. There were few people around, less movement. Neglect was evident everywhere; some of the fields looked like they hadn't been worked in days. Entering the main house, looking about, all was not well. The dust was thick, the floors were filthy, and the beds were unmade. Looking in their closets, all their clothing was missing. The kitchen was an eyesore with grimy pots and pans piled high, and an old black woman that Collin did not know claiming to be the cook.

Just then, Dale Grundy entered the kitchen through the back door.

"Mr. Townsend, I thought it was you that drove onto the property."

Dale Grundy was a tall, lanky young white man, hard working, and loyal as the day is long. If you considered the Townsend Plantation and compared it to a sailing ship, Noah Hancock, the head overseers, would be the captain, and Dale Grundy would be his first mate.

"Grundy…!" Collin proclaimed in a loud surprised voice. "What the hell is going on around here?"

Grundy stood silent and fearful. He knew of Collin's temper, the type to kill the messenger of bad news.

"Don't worry, I just want to know," Collin said in a calmer tone.

Grundy slowly gave his report: "You've been gone for a long time, Mr. Townsend. I didn't know how to get in touch with you."

"Go on."

"At first, everything was the way it always was. Then Mr. Hancock says he got a letter from you saying the harvesting plans needed to change. That's when everything went to hell in a hand basket. Mr. Hancock pushed everyone to their limit. Everyone, freeman or slave, worked sixteen hours each day, sometimes as much as twenty. He said his orders were to harvest every field as soon as possible. Nobody questioned him. We put our heads down, and did our jobs.

"In a fairly short time, we'd harvested all the fields, even one or two I warned were too young. There was nothing left to harvest. As always, Mr. Grimmer came for the weighing. And as always, Mr. Hancock took the payment, got in his wagon, and rode into town to deposit it at the bank. The only difference was Mr. Hancock never returned. At first, I thought he remained in town to blow off a little steam. After all, he'd been working pretty hard lately. A man's entitled to blow off some steam, now and then.

"When he didn't return the next morning, I took one of the horses and road into town. You never know, he might have met with some foul play. I checked all over town. Nobody said they saw him. I even went to the bank. They told me he never came in to make the deposit.

"When I got back to the plantation, I went to his shack. It was then I realized why he took a wagon and not just a horse. All his things were gone. I guess he put them in the back of the wagon and covered them with a tarp.

"With no real leadership, everything went from bad to worse. Slaves started to make a run for it. Everyday more went missin'. The only slaves left are the ones too frightened to run, or they have youngsters, or they're too old. I didn't know what to do. I'm sorry, Mr. Townsend, I just ain't that kind of fellow."

The young man stood there, waiting for Collin's reaction.

He spoke calmly and firmly. "You're fired."

"But, Mr. Townsend…!"

Collin turned, leaving the kitchen. He spoke over his shoulder, never looking back. "You've got one hour to pack your gear and get off my property. If I see your face after that time, I'll shoot you."

Beth rushed behind him, trying to keep up. As far as Collin was concerned, there was nothing left to do other than go upstairs and get drunk.

****

For a full week, Collin never emerged from his bedroom; he didn't eat, wash, or change his clothes. He hardly touched Beth, and when he did it was cold and joyless, sometimes hitting her.

Beth never complained. If anything, she was enjoying seeing him like this. She'd sit at his bedside watching him sleep, reveling in his suffering.

Early one morning, there was a pounding on the bedroom door.

Without opening his eyes or lifting his head, Collin shouted at the door. "Go away!"

Despite his anger, the pounding continued. Beth was about to get off the bed and answer the door when the voice of the new cook, the old woman whose name they didn't know, called through the door from the hallway.

"I'm sorry to disturb ya, Master Townsend, but there be two men downstairs come to see ya." This didn't stir Collin in the least. It was her next sentence that jarred him to his feet, to the chair that held his clothes. "They say they be from the bank."

"Tell them I'll be right down."

"Do you want me to go with you?" Beth asked, smiling up from the bed.

"No, you stay here and keep the covers warm. I'll be right back."

Once dressed enough to look somewhat decent, he rushed out and down the stairs.

There was no way Beth was going to miss this. Jumping from the bed, she grabbed her robe to wrap around her, as she flew out of the room and down the stairs. She heard voices coming from the study. The doors were closed. She placed her ear close. She heard every word.

"Mr. Townsend, I know this comes as a shock; however, there is nothing else we can do. Our hands are tied. When your bills started to mount, we sent word to Mr. Martin, your accountant. Days passed without a word from him; so, we decided to pay Mr. Martin a visit at his office. On arriving, we found his business closed, and after more inquires we learned he left town without leaving a word with anyone. That was when we felt it proper to assess your account at the bank.

"I'm afraid what we found, sir, is the second part and worst of the bad news. I regret to inform you, sir, that your bank account is nearly empty, and we suspect Mr. Martin is the culprit."

There was a brief moment of silence, and then the other man took over.

"To the disbelief of many people, banks are not heartless. Still, we have our job to do. Hopefully, we can find a happy medium where both parties benefit. These debts of yours are high dollar, many, and long standing.

"Mr. Townsend, you and your family have been good costumers for years. We'd hate to lose that. As I said, we are not completely heartless; however, we have a job to do. Now, I must ask you, sir, truthfully, what are the chances of these debts being paid?"

Beth heard Collin speak. "There's not a snowball's chance in hell of them every being paid."

"Was afraid you'd say that," remarked the second gentleman. "You understand if you don't pay your debts the bank can seize all your assets, this home, this plantation, everything you own?"

"Yes, I understand."

Another long silence, then the first gentleman spoke. "I'll tell you what we can do. We'll give you one month to come up with a decent amount. It doesn't have to be the whole amount, just something substantial. From there, perhaps we can work out a monthly payment plan. What do you say to that, Mr. Townsend?"

Collin laughed, "Do I have a choice?"

Beth heard footsteps coming to the door. She dashed up the stairs. She could hear the door opening and Collin speaking. "I thank you gentlemen for this opportunity and your kindness. In the next month, I'll try to come up with your money."

"Good day, Mr. Townsend," the two men said in unison.

"Good day to you, sirs."

By the time the front door slammed, Beth was back in bed, the covers over her head. She pretended to be asleep when Collin entered the bedroom.

He undressed, throwing his clothes over the arm of a chair. He came and sat on the edge of the bed. There was a half filled bottle of whiskey on the nightstand. He filled a large glass up to the brim and began to drink.

"Who was it?" Beth asked, trying to make it sound that she'd just woke, and was only semi-interested, and not prying.

"Some gentlemen from the bank," he answered, as if it were trivial, and nothing to take much notice of.

"What did they want?"

"Nothing, just my blood," he laughed.

In the next instant, he downed the drink, and then poured another, and started on that.

Beth was smiling on the inside. She knew what Collin's answer for any crisis was…to drink himself into a stupor, till all of his worries dissolved in whiskey. And with the help of opium and chloroform, he couldn't fail in his mission.

For Beth, this was the best of times. All she need do was sit back and enjoy his demise. And in the end, before he'd take his last breath, while he is still coherent, she'd tell him the truth, she was the cause of it all.

31

Forgiveness and Restoration

As Beth suspected, Collin did nothing to improve his situation. Many men would take advantage of the given grace period from the bank, lift themselves up by their bootstraps, and give it a go. Even if doomed to fail, they would at least go down fighting. Not Collin, he wallowed in self-pity, proving to Beth what a truly weak man she believed him to be.

He spent his days in bed, drinking and taking drugs, which Beth made sure there was an ample supply. In all their time together, she, like everyone else in Collin's life, robbed from him. Now, she had a pretty penny saved and hidden.

Each day she noticed the difference in Collin. His downfall was clear and imminent. His eyes grew pale, vacant and lifeless. His weight loss was obvious, his frame protruding under his skin like the ribs in an umbrella, His cheeks sunk into his face till you could see the outline of his teeth.

Whenever one of the staff came to check on their master, which was seldom, Beth dismissed them. She allowed no one to so much as see him.

In time, the room was filled with the foulest smell. Collin never bathed, nor did Beth wash him. When he became too weak to use the chamber pot, he began relieving himself in the bed. Beth saw to it the mess was never cleaned, nor the sheets changed. In time, from lying in his own excrement, he began breaking out in sores all over his body, which, without care, became infected.

Every hour on the hour, Beth held his head in her hand and poured a full glass of opium laced whiskey down his gullet. This made him sleep, only to wake later with the sweats, moaning for another glass, which she gladly supplied.

His breathing became labored. To take in a full breath took all his strength, and the sound of liquid in his lungs gurgled as he inhaled and exhaled.

When only a few more days of the grace period were left, it was clear Collin wasn't long for this world. It was only a matter of hours. Beth sat close at his bedside, relishing in every moment.

The sun dropped into the horizon, the room went dark. Beth lit a lamp on the nightstand, keeping the flame low, just enough to make out the contours of his face. His breathing became shallow and sparse. The death rattle was in his throat.

Late in the night, he took a turn for the worst. Beth raised the flame on the lamp to have a better look at him. She sat on the edge of the bed. Her time had come, as his time was ending. Now, was the moment she'd dreamed about, to tell him face-to-face the truth as he takes his last breath.

"Collin?" she whispered.

Not a stir from him.

"Collin?" she said softly, her hand on his shoulder.

His eyes opened to slits.

"Collin, it's me, Beth."

His eyes opened fully. He recognized her.

"Collin, you're dying."

"I know," he said in a breathy whimper. He seemed more alert. "I know," he repeated. "But it doesn't matter."

This caught Beth off guard. "What do you mean?" she asked.

"I know I'm going to die, and it doesn't matter. I'm prepared to die. All my life I've lived on my terms, selfish and sinful. Now, in these last few moments, I've prayed for forgiveness and restoration. I've been released. If I die, it doesn't matter, for I go to a better place, to be with my Lord."

This was not what Beth expected or wanted to hear. Collin was the focus of her revengeful life. She planned to bring him to ruin, confront him at the moment of his death, and laugh as demons took his immortal soul to an eternity of suffering.

Now, Collin was prepared to die peacefully in his bed, waiting on a time without end in heaven.

She could not let this happen.

"Collin, listen to me. You're not going to die. I promise you."

She took the bottle of whiskey from the nightstand and replaced it with a pitcher of water. Carefully, she helped him drink almost a full glass. Then she went down to the kitchen, she prepared warm milk and toast with a sprinkle of sugar in a bowl, brought it up to his room, and spoon-fed him.

Being as careful as possible, she rolled him to one side of the bed and then the other to change the bedding. Using a water basin and a few old towels, she washed him, and dressed his wounds using strips from an old sheet she tore.

When she finished, she brought the blanket up to his chin and brushed his hair.

"You're an angel," he whispered to her.

"Now, no more talk about dying, you hear?" she scolded. "You're going to get better."

With this encouragement and her hand gently stroking his forehead, he slowly began to drift off.

"Enough of such talk, you're going to get well."

And he would, she would see to that. She knew Collin better than he knew himself. Standing at death's door frightened him to repentance. Once he was well, his usual self, the old ways would return, making him worthy once more for hell.

32

Buying Time

"There's a Colored woman out here to see you, sir."

"Tell her to go away. I don't have time."

"She says she's from the Townsend Plantation."

Mr. Argent placed his pen on the desk, turned his chair to face the door.

"Very well, show her in."

Mr. Argent was your typical bank vice president, older than middle age, balding, bloating, fat fingers, and a ruddy face. He was remarkably unremarkable, and easy to dismiss. Only, this was his office, his world, he was in charge, and determined to let you know it.

Beth dressed in her finest; however, it didn't impress Mr. Argent. He knew of her post at the Townsend Plantation and clearly didn't approve. His behavior reflected his condemnation and disgust.

"Thank you for seeing me, Mr. Argent. My name is Beth Hanley and I'm…"

"I know who you are," he snapped. "And I know *what* you are. Shall we omit the formalities and the confines of gracious living, which I'm sure you know little of, and get to the reason for your being here?"

Beth didn't miss a beat, continuing to smile. "Very well, Mr. Argent, may I sit down?"

It was obvious Mr. Argent wasn't going to offer her a seat, and Beth wasn't going to wait for an invitation. She moved forward and sat down.

"I'm sure Mr. Townsend would have liked to be here today; only, he hasn't been feeling well. So, I'm afraid you have me to contend with. As you recall, the bank made a generous offer to Mr. Townsend concerning his debts. He'd like to take you up on your proposal of paying off his debts in monthly installments."

"With interest," Mr. Argent was quick to add.

"Yes, of course," Beth replied. She reached into her purse, taking out a large roll of bills. "I have here the first installment of one thousand dollars."

A surprised look exploded onto Mr. Argent's face. It was not what he expected, knowing Collin's character and shortcomings. He was counting on the month's grace period to run out and for the bank to take possession of the Townsend property.

Of course, Collin had nothing to do with the transaction. Beth was offering her own money, which she stole from Collin, one bill at a time. To accomplish her revenge she would need time, and she was willing to buy it.

Mr. Argent erased the look of astonishment from his face and replaced it with an obviously forced smile. He took up the money that Beth placed on his desk.

"I'll be right back with Mr. Collin's receipt, as well as an agreement to the monthly payments for him to sign."

He didn't bother to count the money, which surprised Beth. She sat alone, when after a few minutes he returned with an envelope and handed it to her.

"Have Mr. Townsend sign the agreement and send it back to the bank in care of me, as soon as possible."

Beth opened the envelope and took out the two documents. She couldn't read, however, Mr. Argent didn't know that.

"Everything seems in order," she said, placing the documents back into the envelope, and rose from her chair. "I'll have Mr. Townsend sign the agreement as soon as I get back and then I'll have one of his men deliver it here before the day is over." She started for the door. "It's been a pleasure doing business with you, Mr. Argent."

She could hear him grumbling behind her as she left the office, this made her smile.

During the ride home, her mind was a storm of ideas. She'd bought herself a month's time, would it be enough? It would have to be; there was no more money.

33

Saint Beth

It was apparent Collin's road back to health was to be long, hard, and bumpy. It took Beth a long time to get him to death's door; it would take just as long to get him up to snuff. It wasn't necessarily a case of trying to get him whole and hearty. She just needed to get him as far away from all thoughts of dying as possible. Being on your last leg makes people consider their next step. Facing eternity forces one to focus inward. A young and fit man when full of vinegar never thinks of such things, only, their own selfish desires. Collin was a classic example. Beth held no doubts that when Collin was feeling his oats he'd want to sow them, not to mention his old ways of sin and debauchery.

The first course of action was to get him off drink and drugs. The wise thing to do would be to wean him off slowly, only, there was little time. So, she took his whiskey and opium away and hid them. It was difficult for Collin. He had seizures, hot and cold flashes, deep muscle pains, hallucinations, and the sweats. Beth stayed by his side day and night, afraid he'd try to kill himself. If not for Beth's care, he never would have made it.

Once he started to look better, she made sure he drank plenty of water all through the day, and that he ate three full meals. It didn't take long for him to gain much of his weight back. When he appeared stronger, she took him for walks, going a further distance each day.

Every night, she would put him to bed like a mother puts down her child.

"Thank you," he whispered one night, as she brought the covers up to his chin. "You've been so kind. If it weren't for you I'd be dead. Bless you, Beth. You're a saint."

Beth didn't reply; she just smiled. "You go to sleep, now. Soon you'll be well."

And so it was, a short time later he was strong and well. How did she know this? Simple, one night when she put him to bed, he reached out and pulled her into bed with him. She spent the night with him, the entire night. That's how she knew he'd recovered.

Though physically stronger, his depression continued. His financial woes were still dangling overhead, and it weighed upon him like a mountain. He learned Beth paid the first of the installments. He was not only appreciative it gave him another reason for adoring her. Still, next month loomed in the distance like a storm cloud off on the horizon coming closer with each day.

Collin walked about the plantation like a lost child, feeling helpless and useless. It is only human nature; most people will try to get away with anything they can. Without direction and a steel fist to force him to follow the right course, the plantation fell into disarray and shambles.

This was when Beth decided to change direction, trying to get Collin to return to his old self, again.

The liquor bottles she'd put out of sight from him, she now took out of hiding and placed throughout the house. The drugs, too, she positioned strategically for easy visibility and access. However, this moved him not. He walked passed the items, ignoring them, as if they didn't exist or were invisible.

Had he turned over a new leaf? Was he truly a new creature in his faith? Beth was betting he wasn't. All that was needed was more time. Except, time was running out, the month was nearly over; the next installment on the consolidated loan would be due.

Again, Beth took matters into her own hands. She searched through the main house from attic to root cellar looking for items of value. There were a few pieces of her jewelry that she could live without, a pair of silver cufflinks that she never saw Collin wear. Along the wall on the staircase were three paintings, not from any notable artists, yet, old and lovely. They were sure to bring in a pretty penny.

Then, while going through Collin's closet, she struck gold, literally struck gold. A small snuffbox, once belonging to Collin's grandfather, surely it would fetch a tidy sum, perhaps enough to pay the full thousand dollar installment.

On the last day of the month, once again, Beth found herself in the bank standing before Mr. Argent.

"Cutting it a bit close, don't you think?" he said sarcastically.

"I made it, didn't I?" she responded with just as much sarcasm.

He laughed, "I never doubted you would. Now, if I remember correctly, the payment is one thousand."

Beth placed the bills down on his desk. With one hand he scooped them up and headed for the office door.

"I'll be right back," he declared.

Alone, Beth's mind reeled. They'd made the payment by the skin of their teeth. She doubted there was enough in that old house to sell to make the next payment. She had to come up with another plan.

"Here is your receipt," he said, placing the paper on his desk where the money once was. He returned to his chair, looking up at her inquisitively.

"Is there anything else?" he asked coldly.

"Mr. Argent, a thousand dollars each month is a great amount."

"I agree, only that's what happens when you live carelessly."

Beth turned to assure the office door was closed.

"Mr. Argent, perhaps we can come to some agreement between the two off us." She said this with as much wanton she could gather, a provocative look in her eyes and smile, all the while stroking her hands along the length of her body.

Mr. Argent laughed loudly. "My dear, are you propositioning me? Well, it's a case of too little, a little too late. I'm an old man."

"I like older men," she replied. "Besides you're never too old to enjoy life."

Again, he laughed. "You have no idea what I'm talking about when I say I'm an old man. True, when I was a young man, I'd revel all through the night, sometimes for days. As for women, I'd sell everything I had for a beautiful woman, including my soul. That's the difference between a young man and an old one. I'm no longer that foolish.

"Do you know what motivates me, now, what I'd sell my soul for? It's money. Why? Because with enough money I do anything I want and get anything I want, and that includes women.

"Now, take the receipt, and go home. I'll see you in a month's time."

He laughed at her, as she left the office. She could hear him laughing, as she walked through the bank lobby and out the front door.

****

Back home, Beth was feeling helpless and hopeless. At dinner, she purposely made sure there was a bottle of wine on the table and one of brandy on the sideboard. To her surprise and dismay, Collin asked for water. She was beginning to have sympathy for the devil, knowing what a hard and difficult job he has.

34

A Spoiled Child

It was a slothful process. Slow and steady wins the race. Wherever Collin was, there was Beth, and wherever Beth was she held a glass of liquor. She never said a word or prodded him to join her. She just continued to drink when around him. Actually, she didn't drink as much as it appeared. Whenever Collin was distracted or looked away, Beth would toss her drink. She needed to keep her wits about her. Besides, anyone who drinks that much throughout the day is going down the path to poor health. However, that was exactly what she wanted for Collin.

If some poor soul, by the grace of God, casts aside their drink it is life renewed - a second chance. Still, it would not be wise for that person to take up employment in a tavern. The atmosphere alone would tempt even a saint to backslide. That was exactly what happened to Collin.

In time, being around Beth and her drinking got the best of him. The golden tan color of the brandy, its aroma, tantalized his eyes and nose till only the taste was missing.

As so many others, it starts with just a taste, the one sip won't hurt me frame of mind. Two is no more harmful than one. Two becomes four, four becomes eight, and eight becomes a bottle. The fact the liquor was laced with opium added to its allure.

In under a week, Collin was back to his usual quota of drink and drugs. The crimson in his cheeks vanished. He was once again pale and pasty, like a ghost. The sparkle in his eyes was extinguished, leaving a cloudy orb in the center of his eye. However, the greatest change in him that gave Beth new hope was his demeanor. He slowly returned to his old ways, a man of few good qualities, a man of selfishness, depraved conduct and appetites.

It wasn't till in the third week of that month Beth realized she'd fully succeeded.

To tell the truth, Beth had had enough of Collin. She needed some time away or she'd scream. So, despite having little money to her name, and Collin's credit no longer good, she decided to ride into town and shop.

It wasn't like the old days. Shopkeepers used to fall over themselves trying to please her. Now, they ignored her like a disease. She kept her shopping to items within her budget, which were few. In the end, she purchased a handful of ribbons just for the sake of saying she bought something.

On her return home, she went upstairs to her room. As she passed Collin's room, she pressed her ear to the door, nothing. She could easily enter, except she was still in no mood for him.

In her room, she laid on her bed, staring up at the ceiling. It was so quiet; she fell asleep with no trouble. Just as she drifted off, a sound brought her back. She heard voices seeping through the door that joined her room to Collin's. The voices stopped, followed by the creaking of his wooden bed, along with moans and groans of pleasure. He had a woman in there.

This made Beth smile. Collin was finally once more on the road to perdition.

She considered remaining in bed, listening, however, the temptation was too great. She just had to know who was in the other room with Collin.

Turning the doorknob as gently and silently as she could, she opened the door. Standing in the doorway, she looked to the bed. The sun poured down on the two lovers, making them the focus of the moment.

There was Collin's pale naked body atop of a pretty dark-skinned girl from the slave quarters. The term *girl* was not an exaggeration. She had not yet seen more than thirteen years.

As quiet as Beth was, Collin sensed someone else in the room. He turned his head, looking over his shoulder. When she saw her, he smiled.

"Beth, darling…come join us."

She forced a smile. "No, that's all right. You have fun. I'll see you at dinner," she said calmly, and then returned to her room.

****

There was another flaw in Collin that you often find in most libertines, and that is irresponsibility, they are truly derelict. They care for nothing and no one not even their own well-being, save for their own pleasure. Collin was a proper and classic libertine. He lived his life unencumbered by morals, rejecting all religious beliefs. The man on his deathbed crying out to God for forgiveness and mercy was no more. He was his old self…Godless.

With his said irresponsibility, the date for payment of his monthly consolidated bill from the bank came and went. It surprised Beth how long it took for the hammer to come down; still, down it came. A week after the bill's due date, Mr. Argent and his assistant appeared at the front door.

"Would you like something to drink, gentlemen?" Collin asked holding up a half-filled bottle of whiskey and his half-filled glass. It wouldn't be noon for hours; yet, it was obvious he was drunk.

They ignored the offer considering the early hour and the seriousness of their visit made it inappropriate.

"Mr. Townsend, why don't we sit down? We have much to discuss."

"Of course, of course," Collin said, gesturing to the seats behind the two men. First, Mr. Argent sat, then his assistant, and then Collin, still holding the bottle and the glass. Once seated, he filled the glass to the brim.

"So, how can I help you gentlemen?" Collin asked as if he hadn't a clue and most likely he didn't.

"Mr. Townsend, perhaps you don't realize the seriousness of our visit?" Mr. Argent asked in a calm and soft voice. "You do know that all your unpaid bills have been consolidated and the bank is in possession of the note."

"Yes, I know that," Collin answered with the innocence of a child.

Mr. Argent continued, "You understand that each month you are to pay an amount that we, you and the bank, have agreed on."

"Yes, of course," Collin replied.

"The payment is due at the end of the month, Mr. Townsend. That date is long passed; this is the beginning of the second week of the new month."

"I understand that, Mr. Argent," Collin responded. "I realize it's a bit late, sir. But what is the matter of a few days between friends."

Mr. Argent leaned forward, smiling, still speaking calmly. "Mr. Townsend, this is business; there are no friends in business. I'm afraid you're delinquent on your payment, and keeping with the contract, which you signed I might add, all your assets become property of the bank. This includes the land and the buildings on it, any equipment, animals, product, and of course, slaves."

Collin took a long drink, spilling most of it; his hands were shaking so badly. He let out a low uncomfortable laugh. "Isn't there some kind of agreement we can come to? I promise I will never be late on my payment again."

"I'm sorry, Mr. Townsend, but it's too late for deals. We've already given you a full week's grace. We agree to allow you one week to vacate. Of course, you may take your clothes and any other personal articles. I also know you own a slave girl that you keep as a mistress. We've decided you may keep her. Other than that, you have one week to leave."

Collin jumped to his feet; his drink fell to the floor. Still holding the bottle, he smashed it against the edge of the fireplace. The bottle shattered in half. Shards fell to the floor. He held the broken bottle in his hand by its neck, pointing the jagged glass edge at Mr. Argent.

"This is the Townsend Plantation!" Collin proclaimed loudly. "It has been in our family for generations. Anyone tries to take it away from me and…" Collin jabbed the bottle towards Mr. Argent. "…and I'll kill him."

Mr. Argent rose from his chair, as did his assistant. They walked to the hall, turned and stood in the doorway. Mr. Argent's voice was firm.

"Collin…! I've known you since you were a little boy when I was your Aunt's banker. You were a spoiled child then, and I never liked you. In all these years, it seems little has changed. You are still a spoiled child. Sadly, you will never become a man. And worst of all you are delusional and have no idea how the world works. You have one week to leave."

"And if I refuse?" Collin demanded.

"Then you will be arrested. The sheriff will come and arrest you. That may be the best thing for you. With nowhere to go, perhaps prison would be a good alternative to wandering aimlessly. You'll have a roof over your head and three squares a day." The smile on Mr. Argent's face grew. "No need to show us out, I know the way." Collin could hear him laughing even after he walked away from the building.

All this time, Beth hid behind the stairs, listening. She stood at the door of the sitting room, looking at Collin. He stood in the center of the room, staring a hole into the floor, swaying back and forth and up and down like a harbor buoy in a storm.

She moved towards him. Her steps on the flooring made him aware of her. He looked across to her through tear filled eyes.

"They're trying to kill me," he said in the tone little boys use when showing their skinned knee to their mother.

Beth approached him, resting her hands on his chest; she gently pushed him back into his seat.

"There…there, everything's going to be all right. What you need is a good stiff drink."

At the bookshelf, she found a bottle of whiskey and a tall glass. She filled the glass and gave it to him.

"Here you go. Don't you worry about a thing, it'll be all right."

She watched him drink down to the bottom of the glass. She poured him another.

Her task was nearly coming to an end. All she had to do was keep him drunk and drugged, and let him wallow in his sorrow, spiraling down into the depths of depression. Only this time, she'd keep a close watch over him. At all cost, maintain and remain away from death's door. This time there would be no last minute deathbed salvation.

35

Downfall

Winter arrived like a lion with its bone-chilling wind and rain, and its gray overcast sky blocking most of the sunlight, a horrible time to be evicted.

A better man would have worked to near death to avoid such a thing, and if he failed, he'd prepare for what was to come, but not Collin. He spent what little time left moaning into a glass. If he was awake he was drunk. His intake of opium was enough to kill a horse; he'd built up such a resistance more was needed. What doctors and morticians call a lethal dose.

Unlike the last time, he went on such a bender he would not be able to drink himself to death. There wouldn't be enough time. He had only a few days before he'd be thrown into the cold, literally.

Without guidance or punishments to keep them in line, the plantation fell into chaos and disrepair. Nothing got done; the overseers did whatever they wanted, as well as the slaves. It takes so long to buildup a property; yet, it takes only weeks to turn it to ruin.

Beth did all in her power to add to the confusion and to Collin's ruin. She made sure liquor and opium was plentiful and always near at hand. Her plan was to keep him in this condition till the end of the week's notice.

The first days passed with no change in Collin or the plantation. At the beginning of the last few days, she was sure there would be no miracles. She would tell him of her part in his downfall and then leave.

As for herself, she held no strategy. She'd made no provisions. It didn't matter to her if she lived or died; only that Collin was doomed.

****

It was three in the morning; the house was dark and quiet. Beth entered Collin's room. It was enveloped in darkness. She could hear his snoring; she followed the sound to the side of his bed. Sitting on the edge, she took a match and lit the lamp on the nightstand.

"Collin…Collin…wake up."

He grumbled and smacked his lips. She shook him violently till he woke.

"Beth, what's happening?"

"I just came to say good-bye," she whispered.

"Good-bye…where are you going?"

"It doesn't matter, as long as it's away from you."

He was wide awake now, his voice loud and cruel. "You can't leave me! You belong to me!"

"I don't belong to you any longer, Collin. Don't you know I belong to the bank, now, just like everything you've ever owned. So, I'm leaving. But before I go there's something I want you to know. I was the one behind all of this. I fed your addictions till you lost all control. I helped your head overseer rob you blind. I helped your accountant steal every penny from your account. I was the one that got you kicked out of the crusades.

"Now, not only have you lost everything, you're a shell of a man with no way of getting back on your feet. Not that you ever were a real man. It made me sick whenever you touched me. You make love like an inexperienced schoolboy. You…"

Beth could have gone on like this for hours; only, Collin wasn't having it. His anger ran through his veins like hot lava. His eyes went wide like a wild animal. He leaped out at her. His hands around her throat, he pulled her to the floor. His full weight on top of her, he began strangling the life out of her.

She fought back as hard as she could; only, he was too strong. She punched up at him, but for him it was like being struck by a pillow. He laughed at her desperate efforts. She opened her fists and began clawing at him; her nails digging long lines into his face. The blood flowed down her arms. However, he was so spellbound with rage, he barely felt it.

Beth felt her consciousness dwindling. A numbing tinkle rushed through her body, as darkness began to cover her like a blanket. If she didn't break free in the next few seconds she would be no more. She desperately flapped under him like a fish on dry land, her arms waving about at her sides. Her hand was under the bed, she felt the neck of an empty bottle of whiskey. Taking a firm grip, she brought the bottle hard against the side of his head. He immediately went limp, falling off her. She took in a long loud breath, and then another.

Getting to her feet, she rubbed the soreness from her neck. Looking down, she saw Collin lying at her feet. He was out cold; the blood poured from the cut on his forehead, painting the side of his face crimson. She touched him to make sure he was still alive. Thankfully, he was.

Everything she'd wanted came true. Smiling, she left the room and went downstairs. Without so much as an afterthought to where she would go, if she needed money, or even a winter coat, she marched out of the house and walked away.

****

It began snowing hard and fast. In no time the ground was a blanket of white that crunched under her feet with each step. All she could think about was her sister. She wanted to see Louise's face one more time. She started walking in the direction of the Tanner Plantation. It would be hours; nevertheless, it was the only image forming in her mind.

In time, everything was snow covered. The sun came up, its light reflecting off the snow, offering light without warmth. The snow was now up to her ankles. She walked all day long; sometimes getting lost and walking in circles; still, she remained resolved.

When it comes to the cold, there is a point when it no longer chills, instead, it burns. Beth was at that place. The sun set, making it all the worse, darkness was all around. Beth came to the realization she might not make the night. She had visions of collapsing, lying in the freezing snow, and dying of the cold by morning. That was when she saw it...the cabin.

It was the same cabin she spent the winter so long ago, giving birth to her child. That being the child that Collin sold before she ever knew if it was a boy or a girl, before she could give it a name.

She couldn't help thinking about her friend, Fanny. How lucky she was to know her own child. Yet, how cruel it was for Collin to steal Fanny's child and give it to her. What a malicious and unforgivable lie.

There was the large padlock on the door of the cabin. Beth brushed away the snow with her feet till she found a good sized stone. Taking it up, she smashed it against the lock. It's amazing when survival is the issue one can gather up more strength than they ever thought possible. It took a few tries; nevertheless, she smashed it open.

The one room cabin was untouched, exactly the way she remembered it, the small kitchen, the bed, and the standing stove in the corner. The room was cold, yet so much more comforting than outside.

There was a small pile of wood and a box of matches next to the stove. Once she got a good fire going, it would be warm and cozy. Opening the stove, she used a short thin stick to move the ashes about, and then she hit something solid. She moved the ashes aside, there was a bulky item in the back. She reached in and pulled it out.

It was small and hard. She held it in her hand, unable to identify what it was; it was so covered with sooth. She blew hard on it, removing the ash. Recognizing what it was, she dropped it, and howled loud like a wounded animal. It rolled across the floor. She remained staring at it, shaking like the last autumn leaf in December. It was a skull. Not just any skull, a human skull, an infant's skull, her child's.

Collin lied. He hadn't sold her child; he'd killed it and threw it in the stove, hopefully after it was dead.

****

The house was dark and quiet. She entered the kitchen, taking the largest sharpest knife she found. Slowly and softly she climbed the stairs. Standing in front of Collin's door, she stared into the wood, the fire within her stoked with each thought of vengeance, the thought of a life taken so early without a ghost of a chance of surviving. To never know what life has to offer.

She sat on the edge of the bed, looking out at him; someone took pity on him, binding his head with bandages.

Getting up onto the bed, she straddled him as if he were a horse. Suddenly he woke, unable to breathe from her weight on his chest. He moaned and groaned for a few moments and then gave up.

Sitting on his chest, she smiled down on him.

"Finding it hard to breathe? Can't say a word? And you don't know why? I can tell you why," she said, a full smile beaming on her face. "It's because I just cut your throat. You'll be dead soon. Not too soon, I'll still have enough time to tell you how I feel. You're mind is a most evil mind. Selling my child from under me would have been a most unforgettable sin, but that wasn't enough, you had to kill it, raising it to an unforgivable sin."

Collin's wide eyes flared with anger. He tried to speak; only a gurgling mixed with mumbled grunts rose from his mouth.

"You can't speak can you? Your throat is full of blood and your lungs are loosing air. It's best to remain silent, than die sounding like a fool."

But his hatred wouldn't let him alone. He tried so hard to curse her with his last breath, although, all he did was spit blood on her.

"You know, Collin, it does my heart good to watch you die like some babbling fool; except, it's not enough. There should be more pain. After all, you never had a problem dishing it out. It's only fitting you experience that before you die."

Getting off of him and off the bed, she took the lamp from the nightstand, opened the bottom half and emptied all the kerosene along the edge of the bed, none on him.

She stood at the foot of the bed where he could see her holding a box of matches. Methodically, almost like a religious ceremony, she took out a single match, holding it out before her.

"Isn't it amazing that some of the smallest actions in the world can be the most hateful and hurtful?"

Striking the side of the box, she lit the single match. She held it for the longest time, till it burned to the nub. Surely, it burned her fingertips. Then she tossed what little was left onto the bed. A circle of flame burst all around the edges.

There wasn't enough strength left in Collin to do anything other than toss about. The flames were high and close; yet, still had not touched him. When suddenly, his nightshirt caught fire, he was ablaze in no time, rolling about the bed in agony.

Beth shouted in hopes he heard her words over his agonizing screams.

"This is just a dress rehearsal for what's to come, Collin. I pray you never grow used to it. May a legion of winged demons carry you to hell!"

****

Beth rushed down the stairs and out of the building. She found a large rock facing the front of the house. She sat down on it, preparing to watch the show, and what a grand show it would be.

The small glow of flames grew from the bedroom and then across the entire top floor. The fire crawled down to the first floor. All the house staff that lived in the main house made it out safely; although, they stood in their nightgowns sadly watching the flames burn what little they owned in the world.

Eventually, the house was engulfed in fire. All the snow within a hundred feet melted. Sitting on the rock, watching, Beth was downright warm.

The fire was so great that when the overseers and slaves came to put out the blaze, there was nothing left to do but stare into the inferno.

Others from nearby farms and plantations came to offer their assistance, only to be caught up in that human pastime - gazing into the flames.

When the bonfire grew so large it was seen all the way downtown, the authorities came to investigate. No one could shed any light onto what happened. One moment everything was calm and quiet, as it is every night. The next minute the dark sky was orange and red.

Nothing was clear till they questioned Collin's mistress, the beautiful Black woman sitting on a rock watching the house burn that they understood what happened.

"I did it, and I'd do it again," she admitted. "He killed my baby and led me to believe it was still alive. I once had a small sense of hope, but all that's been taken away. Now, I know different. It was all a lie. Nothing matters anymore."

As they took her away to the downtown jail, she looked back at the inferno that once was the Townsend home and smiled.

36

Epilogue

No matter what they accused her of, she confessed to it. There were even some other crimes she knew nothing about. These cases needed closure. Beth was the scapegoat; so, they tossed all these sins upon her.

Beth only laughed. "After all, they can only hang you once. So what does it matter."

They kept her in a cell by herself, fearing for the safety of others, as she seemed unstable, and she was, and proud of it.

Her trial was nothing but a formality; so they could put it down on the records as her having a fair trial.

It was not a trail by jury, as the court could not justify that much time and expense frittered away on a Black woman. It needed to be short, sweet, and cheap.

The Prosecution attacked her character. How a mistress is nothing more than and adulterous prostitute and should never be trusted. Yet, at the same time she was accused of being ungrateful for all the good things Collin gave to her for being his mistress.

The defense was silent throughout the proceedings. The only objection he proclaimed was the trial was taking far too long. It seemed the defense, the prosecutor, the judge, and the bailiff were all good friends, and these proceedings were cutting deeply into their socializing lunchtime.

They were all pleased with Beth agreeing to everything they accused her of. Only the procedure forced the feet of justice to drag.

In the end, it all worked out the way everyone, including Beth, expected. She was found guilty on all counts. The penalty: to be hanged by the neck until pronounced dead.

****

The usual time between sentencing to death and the execution was less than twelve hours. Meaning: sentencing in the afternoon, and then hanged the following morning. However, the gallows in the square behind city hall hadn't been repaired for so very long, it was decided to disassemble it, and erect a new one. This was a two-week undertaking, in which Beth's trial was in the middle. So, instead of the usual hanging the following morning, it would be a full week before they could execute her. This was an inconvenience for many, including of all people, Beth. She felt ready and willing. A postponement was not only an inconvenience, it was cruel.

The hours passed slowly, sitting in her cell. Till she was told she had a visitor. She perked up, hoping it was her sister. However, she learned, sister or not, Louise would never receive permission to visit, which only dampened her already dwindled spirit.

The key turned, unlocking the cell. In walked the Reverend Jacob Gaines, her pastor from Bethel Church. Though he was the last person she expected to see, she could only imagine why he'd come. Even though she knew he planned to give her one good ear banging, she was willing to see him.

"So, Beth, how have you been?"

"I've been better," she laughed slightly.

"May I sit down?" he asked.

She pointed to the edge of the bed, "Make yourself at home, Pastor.

When he sat was when she became aware he held his Bible.

"You understand why I've come, don't you?"

"You've come to do your job, Reverend. I can't hold that against you; although, to be honest, you're wasting your time."

"Why is that, Beth, do you think you're not worthy?"

"You should ask that of God. Am I worthy? I suppose I'm as worthy as the next person."

"Then why do you think I'm wasting my time?"

Beth smiled, stood and began pacing the cell, hardly looking at him as she spoke.

"Stop me if I'm wrong, Reverend. As simple as forgiveness may appear, it's an awfully complicated matter. There are rules and regulations that must be followed. Am I not right?"

"I wouldn't call them rules and regulations," he responded. "Everything has a natural course it needs to follow. Such is the case with forgiveness. You must first know you have sinned, admit it to God, ask for forgiveness, and finally repent, swearing never to commit the sin again."

"It's that simple?" she asked.

"Yes, Beth, it's that simple."

"Well, Reverend, you had me all the way until the end. I'd fully admit to God or anyone else willing to listen that I've sinned. There's no denying it. Do I want forgiveness? Of course, I do, who wouldn't? Only, when it comes to repentance, am I sorry for what I've done, no I'm not sorry, which leads us to me swearing never to commit this sin again. I can never feel sorry for what I did, and if given the chance I would do it again, gladly."

"Beth, listen to me, you're talking about your immortal soul."

"Tell me something, Reverend, is lying a sin?"

"Of course, it is. And all sins separate us from God, and is worthy of punishment."

"Well, that's what I'd be doing if I said I was sorry. I'd be lying. So, you see it's a no-win situation. Either way I sin. Either way I lose."

Reverend Gaines knew there was no answer that would satisfy her. His mind was spinning, he couldn't think of what else to say or do.

"Child, there's so little time left. Please, promise me you'll think and pray over it."

"I will," she answered, sincere in her response, only knowing there was no chance she'd change her mind.

"Time's up," announced the guard as he opened the cell door.

Reverend Gaines stepped out. The door slammed with a metallic clang.

"You know how your father used to brag that your family was from African royalty? Well, it's true. I knew your grandparents. It was all true."

He had no idea why he said what he did. Supposedly, wanting to end on a high note; only, Beth remained unmoved.

"Is there anything I can do for you?" he asked, sorrowfully.

"Yes, there is, Reverend. My sister…does she still come to church on Sundays?"

"I see her quit often."

"Please, tell her I love her."

"Surely, I will," he said as the guard guided him away. At the last moment, he turned looking at her one last time. "I'll be praying for you."

"I appreciate that, Reverend." Then she smiled at him. "Isn't it ironic that I did so much to send Collin to hell, and now I'm going to join him."

It broke his heart to hear her talk like that. For her sake, he wanted so much to be strong. When he stepped outside, he clasped his hands in prayer, looked up to heaven, and cried.

****

The new gallows was complete. It was Beth's last day. She'd hang in the morning.

The guard jangled his keys and then tapped them against the bars to get her attention.

"You've got a visitor," he announced.

"Tell them to go away," she replied, knowing it wasn't her sister, and that she was in no mood for another ear banging session with the reverend.

"He says he's your husband."

This caught her attention; she rose from the bed and stood waiting.

The guard returned with Gray.

"I'm sorry, I can't let him in," said the guard, he then turned to Gray. "You've got five minutes." He walked away, jangling the keys against his leg.

Beth and Gray stood silently looking at each other through the bars.

"Well, are you going to say something?" she finally asked.

"I'm sorry," he moaned softly in his throat. "It was all my fault."

Beth laughed, "I'd say you had a part in it, but I wouldn't play the martyr and say it's all your fault. Besides, I'm a big girl; I made my bed, now I've got to sleep in it."

"I wish there was something I could do?"

"And if wishes were feathers, we'd all be tickled. Listen, I've only got a few more hours. If you came to moan and groan, you might as well leave now."

Gray went silent for a moment and then he blurted out what he really came to say. "I loved you, Beth. I still love you. I will always love you."

"I love you, too," she declared, knowing it was not time to hold back.

They stood staring at each other, silent, as if both knew there was nothing else to say.

"Gray, listen, I have something important to tell you. I suppose I could complain about this and that, but when it comes to the facts, you're a good man. I'm going to make a suggestion; I want you to think it over carefully. I want you to look after my sister, Louise."

"Of course, I will," he responded.

"No, Gray, more than that, I want you to marry Louise. She's a good woman and she'll make a good wife."

"I already have a wife," he countered.

"Not for long, you don't. Just think about it, Gray."

Just then, the sound of jangling keys grew louder. The guard returned.

"Time's up."

"Beth…I…"

"It's all right, Gray. Just think about what I said."

The guard took hold of Gray's arm. "You need to leave."

Gray took one last look at his wife.

She smiled, he smiled back.

****

It was early morning. There was no need to wake her, Beth did not sleep. She sat and thought the whole night through. Thinking about what was and what might have been.

There was no last meal, no drums or fanfare, and no last words. They opened the cell, took her by the arms and marched her outside to the courtyard.

The courtyard behind city hall was enclosed by a high wall. It wasn't always like that. There was a time executions were open to the public. The people came for miles to see someone hanged. This was good for commerce, taverns, cafes, and hotels. However, it became costly for the city. Just the expense of security and crowd control resulted in a pricey sum. Therefore, a high wall was built around the courtyard. Only officials and news reporters had permission to attend executions. To appease the public, an excessively tall flagpole was erected in the courtyard. Once a prisoner was pronounced dead, a solid black flag was raised as a public announcement. At first, folks would stand by the wall waiting for the black flag. Except, it was so anticlimactic that in time few people bothered, and finally no one came at all.

Strange how the simple things in life become the most precious when they're taken away. When Beth walked out into the courtyard, she looked up, directly into the sun, feeling its warmth on her face. Taking in a deep breath, she remembered how sweet morning air could be, the sound of the wind, caressing her, singing into her ears.

They rushed her up the thirteen steps to the top of the gallows, placed her over the trap, and bound her hands and feet. The next thing she knew, a sack was placed over her head and a noose around her neck. The world went dark.

****

Meanwhile, outside on the other side of the wall, Gray sat on the ground, staring at the flagpole. He was under the same sun, he breathed in the same air and felt and heard the same wind; only, it all went unnoticed.

"Why is it taking so long?" he said, seemingly cursing the empty flagpole. Then it struck him what an uncaring statement that was. No flag meant she was still alive. Isn't that what he should truly want? Still, it was the unnerving anticipation eating at his bones that made his mind go in the wrong direction.

A wave of guilt washed over him. He had changed so much, lately, and in such a short time. Thinking of his younger self, he wanted to take that young man and beat some sense into him. How could he have been so foolish? It was all pride. The Book of Proverbs tell us: *When Pride comes, then comes disgrace*. He was now buried in disgrace; and it would be a hard undertaking to dig his way out.

Suddenly, he heard a slapping noise. It was the sound of taut ropes hitting against the wooden flagpole. It wasn't the wind; the wind wasn't blowing strong enough. Someone was at the bottom, manipulating the lines.

His eyes glued to the top of the pole. Knowing what he was about to see, his body stiffened and the hairs on his neck stood out. For some strange reason, when he saw the flag rising, it still struck him as a surprise.

When the flag was at full mast, he rose to a standing position. Turning to one side, he reached out his hand, helping Louise to her feet.

"It's over," he said gently. "Come, my dear, we need to go and speak with Reverend Gaines to set our wedding day."

THE END

Michael Edwin Q. is available for book interviews and personal appearances. For more information visit michaeledwinq.com

Other Titles in this series by Michael Edwin Q:

Born A Colored Girl: 978-1-59755-478-4
Pappy Moses' Peanut Plantation: 978-1-59755-482-8
But Have Not Love: 978-1-59755-494-7
Tame the Savage Heart: 978-1-59755-5098
A Slaves Song: 978-1-59755-527-5
Fancy: 978-1-59755-540-1
Wistful: 978-1-59755-563-0
Winnie: 978-1-59755-600-2
Sisters: 978-1-59755-641-5
Death in Savannah: 978-1-59755-616-3
Death in Tallahassee: 978-1-59755-658-3

To purchase copies of these books, visit our bookstore website at:
www.advbookstore.com

Longwood, Florida, USA
"we bring dreams to life"™
www.advbookstore.com

Michael Edwin Q.

www.ingramcontent.com/pod-product-compliance
Lightning Source LLC
Chambersburg PA
CBHW051512260626
47162CB00008B/2930